DOOZER

BURNING SAINTS MC BOOK #5

JACK DAVENPORT

Doozer is a work of fiction. Names, characters, places, and incidents are the products of the author's imagination and are used fictitiously. Any resemblance to actual events, locales, or persons, living or dead, is entirely coincidental.

Cover Art
Jack Davenport

Photographer
Golden Czermak

Cover Model
Andrew England

ISBN: 9798586768896

BURNING SAINTS

Oh, good gravy, this book is good. And I'm not just saying that because he does other amazing things with his fingers!

~ **Piper Davenport, Contemporary Romance Author**

Piper

I couldn't do any of this without you. Literally, my fingers would fall off and I'd be a vegetable.

Brandy G.

Thank you for the million reads and your attention to detail!!! You're amazing.

Gail G.

You're a rock star! Thank you for all your help!

Mary H.

A million thanks! You're an angel.

Carrie Marie and Robin M.

Thank you for the last-minute pitch hits!

For Ziggy

The best club historian the Burning Saints has ever had!

Doozer

About two years ago…

I ARRIVED AT the historic Douglas Hotel an hour late and pulled my bike up to the valet parking kiosk per the instructions on my invitation. I killed the engine, removed my helmet, and was immediately greeted by a skinny man wearing a red vest, holding a clipboard.

"Good afternoon, sir," he said, in an uptight tone. "This area is reserved for valet parking for guests of the Locke, Mancini, and Pratt holiday party."

"Yeah, I'm here for that," I said, pulling the invitation from my kutte pocket and handing it to him."

"You're a guest of *this* party?" he asked, pointing to the invitation, his voice dripping with disdain.

"That's right," I replied, dryly.

I can't say I was surprised at his reaction, considering I was equally shocked when the invitation arrived at the Sanctuary.

The valet looked at my name patch, then to the paper on his clipboard. He ran his bony finger down the page. "I'm sorry, sir but I don't seem to have a *Doozer* on the guest list."

"Believe me, buddy, I'm on it," I said, running out of patience. "Look. I've got my invitation, so just tell me where to park my bike and I'll find the party myself."

"Sir, this event is a black-tie affair," he said, looking me up and down.

"My tux is at the cleaners, what can I say? Listen, man, I'm supposed to be here tonight, and I'm already late, so—"

"Could you be on the list under another name? Perhaps your *proper* name."

My back muscles tightened.

"Check under Mancini," I replied.

"Mancini?"

"Yeah. Marco Mancini. As in Locke, *Mancini*, and Pratt. The guy in the middle is my old man," I said, pointing to the letterhead at the top of the paper. "Like I said. I'm on the list."

"Of course," he said, clearing his throat. "You can park over there." He pointed to the adjacent lot.

"Tell you what. Instead of that, how about I park my bike right over there," I said, motioning to a space on the sidewalk, near the kiosk.

"Well, I…I—"

"That way, you can keep an eye on her for me." I

pulled out my money roll, peeled off two twenties and stuffed them into the valet's hand before he could get another word out. I then pulled into my private space and made my way inside.

The Douglas Hotel was as old as Portland itself and almost as beautiful. As I walked through the lobby, I was met with the usual amount of "stank face" from the hotel's guests and a barrage of "May I help you?" from the staff. Of course, 'May I help you?' is code for "What the fuck is a degenerate biker like you doing in a respectable establishment such as this?" but I didn't give a shit. I was used to the dirty looks and the inevitable "purse clutching" as I walked by that came along with being a tatted-up biker.

I made my way to the grand ballroom and found the festivities well underway. Even though it was barely past six o'clock, the dance floor was already a mass of suits, ties, and cocktail dresses. Not surprising as, in my experience, lawyers did two things to excess. Work and party. That is, except for my father, who was incapable of relaxing. The only reason he took Sundays off was because God commanded it. Even then, he'd always find some reason to sneak off to his home office after church. I was shocked when my sister told me Pop was retiring. I'd never once pictured Berto Mancini leaving his practice and couldn't imagine him with free time on his hands.

Tonight was not only Locke, Mancini, and Pratt's annual holiday bash, it was also my father's retirement party, which meant he'd probably be on edge from all the attention he'd be getting. For all his faults, my father was a humble man, who had no need for "peacocking" as he called it. He referred to my tattoos as "feathers."

I headed to the bar next to the DJ booth in hopes of getting a drink before seeing my old man. The DJ was blasting the typical dance crap specifically designed to help drunk white people find the beat no matter how wasted they got. I hated it but at least it wasn't fucking Christmas music. Not that it mattered much to me as I wasn't planning on staying any longer than I had to. I was here to congratulate my father on his retirement, avoid my mother's annual attempts to get me to go to Christmas Eve mass, and get the hell out of here as soon as possible.

I ordered a Jack and Coke from the bartender and scanned the ballroom for my father while I waited.

"Look what the reindeer dragged in," a voice shouted over the din of the dance music and I turned to see my sister, Carmen, dressed to the nines.

"Hey, sis. You look beautiful," I said, giving her a hug.

"Thank you. I feel like a total dickhead in this dress," she replied.

"I know a lot of dickheads, and you don't look like any of them. Trust me," I said. "You look great. Very…grown up."

"You mean, old."

"I didn't say that, and you don't."

"Well, *one* of us has to dress like an adult," Carmen said with a smirk.

"You're starting to sound like Pop. Where is he?" I asked.

"Sitting over there with Mama, Gia, and Gaga," she said, motioning to the other side of the dance floor.

"Gaga's here too?" I asked, surprised by my very elderly grandmother's presence.

"Of course. It's Pop's big night," Carmen replied.

"She's a hundred years old. This music must be driving her fucking crazy."

"She's ninety-two and without her hearing aids in,

she can't hear anything."

"Lucky bitch," I said.

"Marco!" Carmen shouted, punching my arm. "Don't call our grandmother a bitch."

"I just meant she doesn't have to listen to this shitty dance music all night," I said.

"I'd be more worried about listening to the shit our Pop is gonna give you about how you're dressed."

"Did he see me come in?"

"Why do you think I'm here?" She smiled.

"What? He can't come talk to me himself. He has to send you, now," I said. "Figures."

"It's not like that," Carmen said. "I said I'd come get you and bring you back to the family table."

"You sure there's room for me?" I asked.

"Come on, Marco. Don't be like that," she said.

"Be like what, Carm? He fucking hates me."

"Pop doesn't *hate* you."

"Oh, yeah? Let me ask you something. Were you with him when I walked in?"

My sister nodded.

"When Pop saw me, did he say anything?"

"I don't know, maybe. It's loud in here," she replied, unconvincingly.

"So, he didn't make some smart-ass remark the second he laid eyes on me?"

"I don't know," Carmen said, unable to hide her nervous smile.

"You know, for a lawyer, you're a shitty liar," I said.

"Only because it's you, Marco. I've never been able to lie to you. Even when we were kids."

"What about Gia?" I asked.

"Lie to Gia? Only a million and a half times. But that's usually because I was avoiding an ass beating for using her make up or borrowing her clothes without asking," she said.

"Yeah, I guess you and I never really had that problem. Did we?"

"Jack and Coke," the bartender said, sliding my drink across the bar.

"Merry Christmas," I said, placing a twenty into his tip jar.

"Business must be good," Carmen said.

"We currently have a two-and-a-half year waiting list," I replied.

"You're kidding? That's fantastic. Congratulations," she said, giving me another hug.

"The custom bike business is a lot more work than I thought it would be, but I love it."

"I'm proud of you, baby brother."

"Thanks, sis."

"Now, let's get you to the table before Pop sends out a search party to find us."

I grabbed my drink and reluctantly followed my sister to our table.

I'm the youngest of the three siblings. My sister Gia is six years older than me and Carmen is four years older. Growing up I got along with both of my sisters, but Carmen and I have always been the closest. My sisters would have almost daily epic, knockdown, drag out fights about anything and everything and I would play peacemaker between them. Gia, being the oldest, would usually end up getting her way, which would often leave Carm and I paired up together by default. But no matter what, I always had her back and she always had mine.

To my mother and my sisters, I was definitely "the baby" of the family. My father, on the other hand, had labeled me the "black sheep" by my early teens. Unlike my sisters, I'd never done well in school and had a hard time with anyone in authority telling me what to do. I was fifteen when I first started getting tattoos and riding motorcycles. By seventeen, I'd been kicked out of school, and then out of my home. The night my father put me out on the street, he called me a degenerate, a thug, and a loser. He called my tattoos the "marks of the devil" and told me I would never amount to anything more than a jailhouse snitch. I'd only spoken with him a half-dozen times in the years since and never about anything important. It had been almost a year since our last conversation, which ended poorly, to say the least.

My stomach tightened as soon as I spotted the table. My father was standing at the far end of the table, away from the rest of the family. In front of him was a line of well-wishers and glad-handers which snaked all the way back to the dance floor. Pop had been practicing law in Portland for forty years and within that time had made many powerful friends and allies. He'd also made his share of enemies. Certainly, this line of glad-handers was made up of both.

"So, what do I do, consigliere? Wait in line for the Don with the others?" I asked Carmen in a mock mobster voice.

"Shut up and sit down, Fredo," she replied.

"*Fredo*? No, no, no. You've got it all wrong. Michael was the youngest of the Corleone family children," I corrected her. "I'm Michael."

"Whatever you say. Now go find a seat and practice saying the hail Mary while I gas up the dinghy."

"Damn. You're cold," I replied. "I guess you'll make a great lawyer after all."

Growing up, my sisters and I were obsessed with gangster movies and Godfather II was at the top of the heap. We could hold entire conversations between ourselves using only movie quotes. Much like the Corleone Family both of my siblings followed in my father's footsteps, earning law degrees from Stanford, and were now working for him at the firm. This of course was the path he'd carved out for me as well, but I'd rather saw my left arm off with a sharpened library card than practice law with my father. Unlike Michael Corleone I didn't join the army to escape my father's plans for me. Instead, I pledged my allegiance to the Burning Saints Motorcycle Club. Making my bones as an enforcer on the streets of Portland.

"Marco," my mother exclaimed, rising to her feet as Carmen and I approached the table.

I made my way to her and greeted my mother with a hug and a kiss. Mama was a wonderful woman, who'd devoted her entire life to the church and her family.

"You're late," she said.

"I'm sure he cares," I said sarcastically, motioning to my father who had yet to acknowledge my presence. His attention never once wavering from the impeccably dressed couple standing in front of him. They looked to be around his age and reminded me of Mr. and Mrs. Howell, the old rich couple from Gilligan's Island.

"*I* care," my mother said, reaching up to pinch my cheek.

"Sorry, Mama," I said. "How are you?"

"Your father is driving me crazy. He wants to buy an RV and drive across the country. Can you believe that?"

"An RV? As in recreational vehicle?" I asked, stunned.

"He has some crazy fantasy about fishing in the streams of Montana one day and eating pizza in New York the next. I think he's losing his mind."

"He's probably nervous about retirement," I said, trying to comfort my mother. In truth, I doubted Pop had ever been nervous about anything. Regardless of what he was doing, my father had one setting. Full speed ahead. Damn the torpedoes. If he *did* manage to convince my mother to take this road trip, it would likely be their last. Pop would probably end up driving the RV straight into the Grand Canyon because he was busy arguing with the GPS navigator.

"It's all he talks about. He's on the internet at all hours, looking up various models and talking to dealers. He's got RV fever."

"I'm sure it'll pass," I said. "Besides, are we one-hundred percent sure he's actually retiring?"

Mama smiled and shrugged. "Who knows? I still hear him on the phone, at all hours, talking business. He's probably looking for an RV with an office in it."

"If he finds one with a putting green in it, you're done for," I teased.

Mama looked at me with a panicked expression, and then crossed herself before kissing her imaginary rosary. "Don't speak that evil, Marco," she said.

I laughed out loud, catching the attention of my father, who turned and gave me what could only be described in the loosest legal terms as "a smile," before immediately returning to his guests.

"Is Pop drunk?" I asked, in shock by what I'd seen.

"Marco," my mother chided. "Please don't give your father a hard time tonight. It's his retirement party."

"He's the one who stirs the pot, Mama. Not me."

"Don't act like I don't know my own son. You keep a giant spoon in your back pocket with your father's name on it."

I laughed again, but my mother just looked at me sternly.

"I promise, I'll be good," I said, crossing my heart.

"Does that mean I'll see you at St. Luke's for Christmas Eve Mass?"

My hand went to the back of my neck. "I don't

know, Mama. Maybe, we'll see."

"We'll see? What kind of answer is that? When's the last time you attended mass? Or went to confession?"

"*Confession*? Come on, Mama. Gimmie a break."

"How about I break your backside? You need to confess your sins, and make yourself right with the Lord, Marco."

"Maybe, I'll see you on Christmas eve," I said, trying to sound as non-committal as possible, but Mama was having none of it. Shooting me the mother of all glares until I broke. "Okay, okay. I'll do my best to be there. Okay?"

"Good. Now say hello to everyone else," she said, and I gave her a kiss before making my way down the table.

My grandmother sat quietly. Her eyes transfixed on the DJ's light show. The palms of both her hands lay flat on the table as she bobbed her head along with the pulse of the music.

"She's been that way since the music started," Gia said.

I bent down and kissed my grandmother's cheek. Her eyes met mine and she smiled briefly before turning her attention back to the light show.

"I think she recognizes us less and less every day," Gia said. "But she seems happy and at least she doesn't ask about Pop-Pop as much."

"That's good," I said.

Gaga, who was my father's mother, was suffering from the effects of advanced Alzheimer's. She would sometimes forget about my grandfather's passing and it was a heartbreaking event every time she had to be reminded.

"What do you think about Pop retiring?" I asked, taking a seat next to Gia.

"I think I need a drink," she said.

"So, what's stopping you?"

"The fact I'll be expected to make a speech later and I'm already nervous enough about stumbling over my words like a blithering idiot."

"A speech, huh? Does that mean you're taking the old man up on his offer?" I asked.

"How do you know about that?" Gia asked.

"Just because Pop and I don't talk doesn't mean I don't hear things," I replied.

"Carmen," Gia said.

"Who else would I hear it from?" I laughed.

"What did she say? Was she mad? She was probably pissed off that I made senior partner so quickly, right?"

"Jesus. No," I said. "She sounded happy for you. Are you okay?" I asked, noticing the color quickly draining from my sister's face.

"I think I'm gonna throw up," Gia replied.

My older sister was as "A type" as they came. As much as Carmen and I may have displayed the traits of middle child and baby, stereotypically, Gia was first born, to the core. Overachieving, in charge, and by the book. She was a great lawyer and would no doubt be a worthy successor at his firm. She was also caring, sweet, and far more sensitive than most people would ever know. Gia also had a sensitive stomach and known to hurl at a moment's notice.

"Here," I said, spotting a bottle of champagne chilling in a silver bucket on the table. I removed the bottle and dumped the ice in a nearby potted plant before handing the bucket to my sister.

Gia took the bucket and stuck her face inside. After a few tense moments, she popped out. "All clear. False alarm," she said, handing the bucket back to me with a smile.

"Marco," my father's voice boomed, and I turned to see him standing behind me, arms extended, smiling. If I didn't know any better, I would have said he looked happy to see me.

Trouble

I STARED IN amazement at Dr. Sinofsky's massive fish tank. It held three hundred gallons of water and dominated almost an entire wall of his office. I watched as various brightly colored, oddly shaped fish swam busily within the safety of their predator free environment. Some fish swimming tightly together in synchronized order, while others cruised alone.

Of all our donation pickup spots, this was by far my favorite, and this time of year meant weekly visits instead of our usual once a month schedule. Usually, I avoided dentists' offices at all costs, but I loved coming here. Mostly because Dr. Sinofsky's donation barrel was always full of brand new, top of the line, toys. I suspected the good doctor himself was largely responsible for this. Secondly (and selfishly), I loved looking at his aquarium. I swear I'd do it for hours if I could. Cowboy was always sweet enough to schedule Dr. Sinofsky's office as our last pickup of the day and instead of our normal "run and gun" operation, he would park the truck so I could stay a while.

"Where are Bonnie and Clyde?" I asked, noticing the absence of Dr. Sinofsky's prized Discus fish.

"I wondered how long it would take you to notice," he replied with a grin.

Over the years of visiting his office, Dr. Sinofsky had taught me all about fresh-water tropical fish of South America and Africa. Much like their ocean-going cousins, these fish were exotic and mesmerizing to observe, but required much less tank maintenance than saltwater setups. I'd especially become fascinated by the Discus fish of the Amazon river, who's bright blue and orange colors glowed like neon. According to Dr. Sinofsky, Discus were as difficult to breed and keep as they were beautiful. He'd been working for almost two years, without success, on mating Bonnie and Clyde.

"I have one more gift for you," Dr. Sinofsky said, pulling a small, wrapped package from his coat pocket.

"This load's already full, Doc," Cowboy said, while loading the overflowing barrel onto the hand truck. "You put anything more in here, and my back may not be able to take it," he joked.

"This one isn't for the kids," Dr. Sinofsky said, handing the package to me.

"For me?" I asked stunned. I couldn't remember the last time anyone had given me a gift and I couldn't imagine what would have possessed Dr. Sinofsky to do so.

"Well, don't leave me in suspense, go on," Cowboy said, his Texan accent still evident even though he'd been in Portland for nearly twenty-five years.

"It's not Christmas yet," I said, the heat of embarrassment creeping up the back of my neck. I wasn't a big fan of being the center of attention. Even when among those I liked the most.

"I'd love for you to open it now as well," Dr. Sinofsky said sweetly.

"I can't say no to you Dr. Sniffy," I said, using the nickname his younger patients called him. Dr. Sinofsky was as far as I could tell, a saint. For two days out of every week his pediatric dental practice provided free care for underprivileged children in Portland, and he sat at the head of one of the largest charity fundraising committees in the area. Our club, Bikers for Kids, had worked with him for years and considered him to be our very own bow-tied mascot.

I carefully began unwrapping the box with Cowboy and Dr. Sinofsky looking on.

"Aw, for fuck's sake. Before next Christmas, shall we?" Cowboy teased.

"Shut up. It's my present and I can open it as slowly as I'd like," I replied.

After removing the wrapping, I could see the gift was an over-the-counter pregnancy test, still sealed in its original packaging, and card which read, "It's a Boy! It's a Girl! It's a Girl! It's a Girl! It's a Boy! It's a Boy! It's a Girl! It's a Boy…"

"Wait," I said excitedly. I turned to the aquarium and did a quick scan. "Bonnie and Clyde?" I held up the pregnancy test. "Does this mean…?"

Dr. Sinofsky smiled wide and his eyes lit up. "Mommy and daddy are resting comfortably at the private maternity ward, also known as my tank at home. Bonnie lay somewhere around two hundred eggs, which Clyde successfully fertilized. This time around Bonnie finally managed to successfully clean and guard her eggs, and now has sixteen thriving fry."

"Congratulations," I squealed and gave Dr. Sinofsky a hug. "I can't wait to see them."

"I knew you'd be as excited as I am. You're always so kind to me. Letting me talk your ear off about my fish."

"This is the best present ever. Thank you."

"Well, that's not the whole gift. Don't you see?"

"What do you mean?"

"Once the fry are a little bigger, I'd love for you to choose a pair of your own. I have a tank for you as well," he said excitedly. "You seem to have such a genuine curiosity and affection for these Discus, and I'd love for you to know the joy of raising a pair of your own."

I'd already been touched to the core that Dr. Sinofsky had included me in his good news, but this was too much. My eyes began to well up, but I did not allow myself to cry. I'd learned to stow that shit away years ago.

"That is the sweetest gift anyone has ever thought to give me, and as much as I'd love to accept it, I can't."

"Why not?" He asked.

"I don't have a permanent place to keep 'em. I have a room here in Portland, but I'm on the road most of the year, and when I'm not, I'm usually crashing on someone's couch."

"Speaking of the road. We'd better get back on it soon. I'll go take this out to the truck and wait for you to finish up with the Doc," Cowboy said, before adding, "Merry Christmas and thank you again. As always, the club appreciates your donations but not as much as the kids do."

"Always happy to give, Cowboy. Be safe out there

and remember to floss."

Cowboy left and I thanked the doctor once more for his thoughtful gift.

Dr. Sinofsky turned his attention back to me. "Next time you're here you can pick out your pair and I'll keep them in the community tank. Should you ever find yourself settled down in one place for a while, I'll have your tank set up and they can go home with you. You just let me know."

Must not cry. Must not cry. Must not fucking cry.

"Okay, I'd better go help Cowboy. That barrel looked heavy and his back isn't what it used to be," I said and made a hasty retreat before I completely lost it.

Dr. Sinofsky's dentist office was in a small strip mall right next to a popular record shop called Village Vinyl. As much as I appreciated much of the music they promoted, it was the type of hangout I tended to avoid as I had little tolerance for whiney suburban kids.

Immediately upon exiting Dr. Sinofsky's office, I was hit by a huge cloud of cigarette smoke. I turned to see two hipster dudes puffing away directly outside the entrance of the record store. Their backs were turned to me and they were laughing loudly. Smoking so close to the building's entrance was not only in clear violation of Oregon's ten-foot rule, but extremely douchey considering their proximity to a pediatric dentist office. As I passed, I could see they were both wearing Village Vinyl staff shirts.

I despised the smell of cigarette smoke, and normally would have already told them off, but today's visit with Dr. Sinofsky had put me in the Christmas spirit and I wasn't about to spoil my good mood by even acknowledging these thoughtless assholes. Walking by, I said nothing. At least that was the plan. Until one of them flicked a lit cigarette butt onto the ground directly in my path.

I stopped dead in my tracks and my head snapped to the pair, who were completely oblivious to my presence. That was about to change.

"Excuse me," I said, several times before finally getting the attention of the village idiots.

"Yeah?" the butt flicker asked, in a disinterested tone.

"I think you dropped something," I said, giving him the opportunity to act like a decent human being and pick up his litter. "Plus, it would be great if you didn't smoke so near the entrance of Dr. Sinofsky's office," I added.

He glanced down at the smoldering butt before turning back to his co-worker without a word.

I felt the Christmas spirit rapidly draining from my body.

"Hey," I said. "You flicked your filthy butt on the sidewalk, right in front of me."

"I'm *sorry*, okay," he replied without turning around.

"You don't sound sorry, and the butt is still on the sidewalk," I said, trying my best to keep my cool. Nothing made my blood boil faster than a bully. The fact that this bully was also a litterbug and an entitled prickwad made me burn twice as hot.

"Never mind, then," he said, his back still to me. "I'm not sorry, *bitch*."

His co-worker laughed as I reached my hand into my jacket pocket.

"I don't give a shit if you are or aren't sorry, asshat," I hissed. "You're gonna come pick this cigarette butt up."

This got the litterbug's full attention, and he marched right up to me as his co-worker stood by, snickering.

"What are you? The fucking trash police or something? How you gonna prove that's even mine?" he asked through a menacing grin. His nametag merely inches from the tip of my nose. The stench of his cigarette breath pouring down on me.

"Tony, is it?"

He nodded.

"Tony, you'd better back the fuck up, and pick up your cigarette butt, now," I growled.

"Or what?" he challenged once more. It would be his last.

I leaned in closer, casually removing my hand, now fitted with brass knuckles, from my pocket. "Wrong answer," I whispered.

Tony's height advantage and our proximity made it easy to deliver a clean inside shot, straight up the middle. My armored fist connecting with his jaw, dropping him straight on his ass, blood pouring from his mouth.

Tony's little toady co-worker bolted inside the store. No doubt to call security or the police.

I grabbed a stunned Tony by the hair, pushing his head down to the ground. "Does it look familiar now or do you need a closer look?" I asked, picking up the still smoldering butt, and holding it to his face.

"No," Tony whined through what was likely a shattered jaw.

I moved the butt closer, inching the smoldering end toward his eye. "How 'bout now?"

Cowboy rounded the corner and bellowed, "Get the fuck off him!"

I scrambled to my feet and slid the blood-covered brass knuckles back into my pocket.

"That bitch hit me," Tony slurred.

"Did I ask you a fucking question, pecker head?"

Cowboy growled down at the bleeding man.

Tony shook his head, and wisely kept his broken trap shut.

Cowboy was normally a sweetheart, but when he was pissed at you, you could feel it in your bones. He wasn't the kind of man who demanded respect, but rather commanded it by the way he handled himself. Both his words and presence carried weight.

"Get in the truck, now," he snapped at me.

I didn't argue, scrambling into the warmth of the cab.

Twenty minutes later, Cowboy climbed in beside me, started the truck's engine and without a word, drove off. For almost twenty minutes we rode in complete silence until I couldn't take it anymore.

"Would you please just yell at me or something?" I begged. "I can't handle the silent treatment."

Cowboy looked at me for a second then set his eyes back to the road.

"Come on. Say *something*," I begged.

"What do you want me to say, Trouble?" he growled. "Should we talk about how much cash it's gonna cost the club to pay that guy's medical bills and keep him from pressing charges? Or about the three years' time you'd do just for having those knuckles, not to mention what you just did with them."

"No one was around."

"Except the six security cameras that no doubt caught everything from several different angles," he pointed out.

"I'm sorry, but that guy—"

"You wanted me to say something, didn't you?" Cowboy snapped, checking his side-view mirror, before pulling the truck to the side of the road. He turned on the hazard lights then faced me. "Do you remember the story I told you when you patched into the club? The one about choosing what kind of person you're gonna be for the rest of your life?"

I nodded. "The one about the wolves, right?"

"That's right. What do you remember me telling you?"

I cleared my throat, feeling like I'd been called to the front of the class by a stern teacher. "You told me that everyone has two wolves living inside them. A good one and a bad one."

"And which wolf wins in the end?" Cowboy asked softly.

"The one you feed," I replied.

"No matter what that guy did back there, was it worth you risking your freedom? Or beating him to death?"

"I only hit him once," I protested.

"And you know damn well sometimes once is all it takes. Plenty of bar fights land people in prison or the morgue."

I blushed. "I know."

"And I know you're smarter than how you acted back there, so you've gotta tell me what the hell you were thinking by going off on that guy like that? When I left, you were all smiles. I came back to fetch you because I thought you'd fallen into one of them fish tanks," Cowboy said, his smile finally returning.

"I fed my bad wolf. I'm sorry, Cowboy. I really am."

"I know you are, and I appreciate that, but sorry don't make things right."

"Are you kicking me out of the club?" I asked, breaking into a cold sweat.

"No, dummy. I'm asking if you're okay. I haven't seen this side of you in quite a while and I'm worried."

"I'm okay," I lied. "That guy, Tony, just set me off, I

guess."

What I didn't want to tell Cowboy was how much I hated this time of year, and how cigarette smoke didn't just bother me. It triggered me. I didn't want to burden him with my "daddy issues" when I knew the club and kids needed his full attention right now.

Christmas was the busiest, and most important time of year for our club. Bikers for Kids earned more in donations between November first and New Year's Eve than the rest of the year combined and doubled. We were also most visible in the community around the holidays and were to be on our best behavior when in public. For many BFK members, myself included, the club provided a shelter from a turbulent past. For some of us that past is far in the distance, and for others, it's staring at us from the rear-view mirror. Normally, I looked forward to the distraction of this busy season as it helped keep my mind occupied. It was easy to avoid focusing on my own pain when I had so many other people and tasks to keep me busy. But so far this year's holiday hustle had failed to distract my demons and I felt myself missing my dad even more than usual.

"Did you really clock him over a cigarette butt?" Cowboy asked.

"He flicked it right at me and acted like I was the one with the fuckin' problem."

"Do you have a problem?" Cowboy asked. His voice full of concern.

"Come on, man. What are you, my therapist?"

"I'm your friend, I'm your president, and I've ridden with enough men to know when one of 'em's got a hell hound on their trail."

"Well, there's your mistake. You've only ridden with men," I joked, attempting to deflect.

"Have I ever treated you any different because

you're a woman?" he asked.

"No," I admitted.

"Then how 'bout you don't treat me any different because you are one."

"Fair enough," I said.

"Besides, I'd like to think we've got enough miles together to where I can tell if somethin's stuck in your spokes."

"You probably know me better than anyone, Cowboy," I said, softly.

"Hey, kiddo," he said, using his most affectionate nickname for me. "Is this about your old man?"

I nodded, and before I could stop them, tears began to stream down my face. "I think it was the cigarette smoke. The smell brought back some bad memories and sort of set me off, I guess. I really am sorry, Cowboy. I'll work off the money to pay for that guy's medical bills. Whatever it takes to make us even."

"Look at me," Cowboy said, lifting my chin to meet his eyes. "We're even, right here, right now. I've got your back, one hundred and fifty percent. You got that? My main concern is for you."

"I'm straight," I said, wiping the tears from my eyes. "Like I said that guy just set me off, is all."

"Then we've got some work to do on your anger management skills," he said with a chuckle.

"And you've gotta work on your math skills. Specifically, how percentages work."

"Okay, how about we solve this little math problem? If Trouble has one illicit piece of weaponry in her pocket and she gives it to Cowboy. How many does she have left?" he asked, holding out his hand.

"None," I replied, sheepishly, pulling the brass knuckles from my pocket and handing them to him.

"*Are we sure*?"

"One hundred and fifty percent," I replied.

He laughed, turned off the hazards, and pulled back onto the road.

Doozer

"I'M SO GLAD you could make it tonight. *Buon natale*," my father said in an uncharacteristically cheery tone.

"Merry Christmas to you too, Pop," I replied, caught off-guard by his unexpected display of warmth.

My father turned to my sister. "Gia, can you do me a favor and go say hello to Mr. and Mrs. Garcia? They were asking about you earlier and I told them you'd stop by their table. They're seated next to the ice sculpture."

"Sure thing, Pop," Gia said, before turning to me. "See you later, Markie," she said, using the childhood nickname reserved only for my sisters.

"Did you get something to eat?" Pop asked. "The food this year is dynamite. I finally got Henry and Karl to agree to having Marconi's cater. Who knew it would only take me retiring to get my partners to finally go along with my choice?"

"No, I just got here about ten minutes ago," I replied.

"Oh, yeah. I think I saw you come in," Pop said, lying far more convincingly than Carmen had.

"Oh, yeah?" I asked and waited for him to unload on me about how I was dressed, showing up late, or whatever the hell else he wanted to get off his chest.

Instead, all he said was, "I sure am glad you're here, son," and, then he hugged me.

My father fucking hugged me.

Now I knew he must be drunk. I'd never seen him drink more than the occasional glass of red wine with dinner at Vincenzo's, and he didn't currently smell like booze, but it was the only explanation. Either that, or he was dying.

I froze in place, unable to process what the hell was going on. In my entire life, I could only remember receiving one hug from my father. When I was ten years old and broke my arm after falling out of the treehouse I'd built all by myself. Looking back, he was probably trying to keep me from going into shock. It was a long fall and a bad break.

"Happy to be here, Pop. Congratulations on your retirement," I said, awkwardly pulling away. "Who would have thought we'd see the day, huh?"

"I'm looking forward to it," he replied. "Now I'll have the time to travel the country with your mother."

"Yeah. She mentioned you want to get an RV," I said, barely able to process what was happening.

"Not 'want to get.' We're going to get one," he said, excitedly. "I'm still deciding on the exact model but that's okay. I have a little time before I have to make the final decision."

"Why's that?"

"Now that Gia is ready to step up, and my client list has been handed over to the other partners, I have a project here in town that I can turn my full attention to."

I knew there was no way my father could stop working.

"You're gonna take on a new case, now?" I asked.

"It's less of a case and more of a...passion project, and it's far from new. This is something I've needed to tend to for quite some time."

"Wow," I said, surprised by the passion in Pop's voice. Whatever my father was taking on had him genuinely fired up. "I look forward to hearing about it," I said. Truthfully, I couldn't have cared less about whatever it was he was into, but I was happy to have his focus directed on anything other than me.

"Oh, you'll hear all about it very soon." My father placed his hand on my shoulder and smiled once more. This time when he smiled the hair on the back of my neck stood up. "Now, if you'll excuse me, I must get back to my guests or I'll be here all night. It really is great to see you, Marco," he said, heading back to his receiving line, before adding, "I'll talk to you soon."

"You will?" I asked, but he'd already disappeared back into the fold.

"What was that all about?" Carmen asked as she rushed to me. She'd obviously been watching my father and me from the sidelines and seemed as shocked as I was.

"I have no fucking idea," I replied. "He hugged me, Carm."

"I saw that."

"Is Pop sick? Is he dying?"

"Don't say that," Carmen said, crossing herself.

"I'm telling you, something's up. He was talking about working on some lifelong project now that he's retired. He was beaming. Do you know what the hell he's talking about?"

"No, but maybe Gia does. She's way more in the loop regarding his cases."

"I'm not sure this has to do with the firm. He said it was personal."

"Maybe it has to do with managing Gaga's estate."

"It's probably nothing. I think I'm just weirded out because he was nice to me."

"Well. That is *really* weird."

"Why are *you* so shocked? Earlier, you were trying to convince me that Pop doesn't hate me."

"I said he doesn't hate you. Not that he *likes* you."

"Well, apparently we're best buds as far as he's concerned."

"Does that mean you're gonna stick around tonight?"

"For a little while, then I really do have to go. But I've gotta hit the head, first."

"Okay," she said.

I smiled, kissing her cheek before heading to the bathroom. I did my thing, let out a few choice words when I noticed there were no paper towels, and walked out of the bathroom wiping my wet hands on my jeans to try and dry them. "Fuckin' hippies."

I rounded the corner and noticed my father talking jovially with a few of his usual cronies, and a man I would never have expected to see him with. Judge Reginald Snodgrass or Judge Snotty as my father always referred to him.

I headed back to my sister who frowned at me as I approached. "What's wrong?"

"Why the fuck is Dad all chummy with Judge Snotty?"

She shrugged. "I think they're working on something together. He's been around the office a bunch lately."

"Carmen, Dad hates Judge Snotty and everything he represents."

Judge Snodgrass was notorious for his shady sentences and back-door dealings with all manner of illicit individuals. My father was honest to a fault, at least as honest as a lawyer can be, and had made more than one, or twelve, motions to recuse the judge when he was presiding over any of Dad's cases.

"I think with Dad retiring, they buried the hatchet."

I frowned. "Dad doesn't bury hatchets, Carmen, unless he's aiming one at me."

She sighed. "He's not that bad."

"No, you're just his little girl, so you're blind to what an asshole he can be."

"*Or*, you're being too alpha male to set your ego aside and entertain the possibility that Pop's changed."

I grunted. I loved my sister to Mars and back, but she'd been sheltered to the point of ignorance and that bugged the shit out of me.

"I should head out," I said.

"That's it?"

"Sorry, sis, I have a club Christmas party to get to."

"Tonight?" she asked.

I raised an eyebrow. "Why is that strange? We're at a party right now."

"I know, but this is…"

"This is what?" I challenged. "A normal, corporate sanctioned, socially acceptable, holiday party and MCs are only allowed to hang out with strippers and sacrifice goats."

“I didn’t mean it like that, I was just surprised, that’s all.”

“I expected to get shit from Pop and Mama about leaving tonight, but not from you.”

“Hold on, Marco. Just because you didn’t get to have a fight with Pop tonight doesn’t mean you get to start one with me.”

“I’m sorry, Carm. You’re right.”

“Do you have to go? I miss you. Will we see you at mass this year?”

“First Ma, now you?” I laughed. “I promise I’ll call on Christmas, but I really do need to hit the road.”

Tonight, the Burning Saints were to be the guests of the Dogs of Fire. A local MC we’d recently become friendly with. Minus had made it clear to all of us that attendance was mandatory. No excuses. And, unlike my father, I cared about disappointing or disobeying my club president.

* * *

I was deep into my second glass of Jägenogg, the Burning Saints’ traditional holiday concoction, and I’d only been at the Dogs’ party for an hour. The celebration was well under way and a group of us were playing nine-ball in the pool room. I was all smiles on the outside but the conversation with my father had my head all twisted up. He was up to something. I could feel it in my bones.

The second I’d walked into the club, I’d tracked down our resident finder of all things dark and dirty, pulling him aside.

“What’s up, little man?” Kitty asked.

Kitty was a giant and despite the fact I was over six feet tall, he’d always called me ‘little man.’

“Need you to do some diggin’ for me on someone.”

He clapped his hands, then rubbed them together. “Do I get to fuck someone up?”

"Don't know yet."

"Whatya got?"

I gave him all the information I knew on Judge Snodgrass, then gave him information about my dad, without giving too much family shit away, trusting that if there was something to find, Kitty would find it.

"I need to find anything that links Snodgrass to my father. Business or personal."

"Leave it with me," he said, and walked away.

My gut churned with unease, but thankfully, I had some drinking and pool playing to do to help take my mind off my father for a while. After a short while I found myself in an epic Saints Vs. Dogs nine ball battle.

"You keep saying you're gonna run the table, but so far all you've done is run your damned mouth," I said, trying my best to get under my opponent's skin.

"Last I checked, I'm up by one game, fool," Sparky replied as he lined up to sink the nine ball.

Not only was Sparky a member of the Dogs of Fire, but he was also the son-in-law of their club's president, Hatch. Hatch just so happened to be Cricket's big brother, the old lady of our president, Minus.

Hatch and Minus had a shady history and that shady history included Hatch maneuvering Minus's exile to Savannah, Georgia over ten years ago. I got the impression, that even though the hatchet had been buried, the handle was still visible in the dirt in case one of them needed access to it.

"Yeah, but we'll be tied once you miss this shot," I goaded.

"Hey, kid, I don't rattle," he replied, quoting Paul Newman from *The Hustler*, a favorite of wannabe pool sharks the world over. Sparky and I may have worn different patches, but we were clearly cut from the same cloth when it came to billiards. In fact, I think we'd spent more time shit-talking during this game than we had playing.

"Okay, Fast Eddie. A hundred bucks says you blow it," I said, taking a sip of Jägenogg.

"Aw, man. How can you drink that shit?" Sweet Pea, my Road Captain, asked from his seat at the bar. His face twisted in disgust.

"What do you mean? It's not Christmas time until I down my first glass of Warthog's holiday specialty," I replied with a smile.

Sweet Pea made gagging noises and I laughed.

"Five-hundred says I make the shot," Sparky said, ignoring the cross-chatter between my teammate and me.

"Shit. If you're just gonna give your money away, why not make it an even grand?" I retorted.

Sparky paused and stood up straight. "You know what? I'll take that bet."

"Babe," Poppy said cautiously.

"No, no," he said, waving her off. "I've got this."

Sparky nodded and returned to the table, bent down, and eyeballed his shot one last time. The nine ball was frozen to the rail and the cue ball was in the worst possible position. To sink the nine would be tricky in and of itself, but to do so without scratching would be nearly impossible. Unless, of course, Sparky was a far better player than he'd been letting on.

After a few ghost strokes Sparky took his shot, and my heart momentarily stopped as the nine-ball sank perfectly into in the corner pocket. Unfortunately for Sparky, his stroke also sent the cue ball flying off the table and into the air. I watched, in slow motion, as the ball hit Sweet Pea square in the sternum with a dull thwack. Sweet Pea's hand went to his chest and he winced in pain.

"I'm sorry, man," Sparky said, setting the pool cue on the table and raising both hands in the air. The universal sign for 'I'm not looking for trouble.'

Sweet Pea shot Sparky a death glare. His nostrils flared like a thoroughbred and the veins in his massive arms popped as he took a step towards Sparky.

"Hey, Captain," I said, now concerned for Sparky's safety. "It was just an accident."

"Accident or not…" The furrow in Sweet Pea's brow deepened and he continued his terrifying stare down. "That was funny as shit," he said before erupting into a fit laughter.

Sparky shook Sweet Pea's hand before handing me a roll of bills.

"It's all there," he said, handing me the cash.

"I'm sure it is," I said, before downing the last of my Jägenogg.

"Alright, we're tied now. Rack 'em up," I said, turning around just as Maisie, the Dogs' First Old Lady, showed up with a smoking hot brunette at her side. She looked to be about my age, was dressed in full riding leathers, and the closer she got, the more beautiful she got. Once they reached us, I could read the name on the young woman's patch, "Trouble."

No shit.

Doozer

TROUBLE WAS, WITHOUT a doubt, the sexiest woman I'd ever seen in my life.

"It's nice to see you again," Sweet Pea said, greeting Maisie with a hug.

"It's wonderful to see you as well, love. Happy Christmas," she said, her British accent adding even more Christmas cheer to the room. "This is Trouble," Maisie said sweetly. "She's with Biker's for Kids. We've just been talking outside and I think she's the most adorable thing ever."

Adorable nothing. She was pure molten hotness that had been poured into leathers.

I scrambled for a smooth way to introduce myself to Trouble as Maisie introduced her to our group. "Trouble, this is Sweet Pea, Sparky, and my daughter, Poppy. And this is Doozer."

"Hey," Trouble said, in a friendly, but guarded, tone.

"'Sup," I said, giving her a casual chin lift. Instantly feeling like a total dickhead.

'Sup? Real fucking smooth.

Thankfully, Poppy chimed in, stepping right over my awkward moment. "Merry Christmas," she said, cheerily. "We're so glad you and the rest of your club could be here with us today."

"Thanks," Trouble said, her eyes nervously going to the floor, before adding, "and Merry Christmas."

"Right, well, I'll leave you all to get to know one another," Maisie said. "Although, I'm afraid I do need Poppy's assistance in the kitchen. I have a bit of a pie situation to sort out."

"Pie? I love pie," Sparky said, and Poppy elbowed him.

"Yeah, honey, we all *know*," she said. "Come on. You can help, too."

With that, Sparky disappeared to the kitchen with Poppy and Maisie, leaving Trouble alone with me and Sweet Pea.

For exactly five seconds.

That's how long it took for Sweet Pea to check his watch, whistle, and say, "Well. I gotta, uh... go help Minus with, uh that… thing," and walk away. He may have been a great Road Captain, but he was complete shit as a wing man. Trouble shot me a nervous glance and tucked her hands into the pockets of her skin-tight pants. Pants I was already envisioning getting into.

"There's a full bar over there. Can I get you a drink?"

"No, thanks. I'm not much of a drinker."

"So, you ride with Biker's for Kids?" I asked, hoping she wouldn't bolt on me. It wasn't too often you'd run into a female patch, and I'd certainly never seen one as beautiful as Trouble.

"Yeah," she replied, barely making eye contact. "Cowboy and I hooked up a little over three years ago."

"Oh," I replied, disappointed. "I didn't know that you were Cowboy's old lady."

"What?" she exclaimed, her voice finally rising above a whisper. "Ew, no. Cowboy's like a hundred years old."

"Shit, I'm sorry," I said, breaking into laughter. "It was just, you said you guys hooked up—"

"I meant Cowboy and I *connected* over three years ago," she said, trying but failing to hide a smile.

I raised an eyebrow. "So, you don't have an old man then?"

"I have a *gun*," she replied.

"Hold on. I think I got off on the wrong foot, here. To be honest with you, my brain is a little scrambled right now. It's been a strange evening, but you seem like an interesting person and I'd like to have a real conversation with you."

She narrowed her eyes but didn't respond. She also didn't walk away, so I tried again.

"Can I have a mulligan?" I asked.

"It's a free country. You can drink whatever you want," Trouble replied, and in that moment, I knew without a doubt that I was fucked. Not regular fucked, mind you. I was royally fucked. I was royal family fucked. I was the crown jewels shoved up my Tower of London fucked.

"No, a mulligan isn't a drink it's a golf term," I said, unable to hide my smile. "It means a do-over."

“Don’t laugh at me because I don’t know old man shit, like that,” she said.

“Is golf old man shit?” I asked.

“Don’t get all offended. What, are you a caddy or something?”

“The only golf I’ve ever played was in high school with my buddy, Munyon, and it was mini golf.”

“What the hell is a Munyon?” Trouble asked.

“Answer my question first,” I replied. “Can I have a mulligan?”

“I don’t know, *can* you?”

I rolled my eyes. “*May* I have a mulligan?”

“Why do you need a mulligan?”

“You came into the room in the middle of a bunch of macho bullshit, caught me completely off guard, and I think I came across like…kind of…a…”

“A douche,” Trouble provided.

“See, look at that,” I said with a smile. “We’re already completing each other’s sentences.”

Trouble struggled with only minor success to hide a smile, but she wasn’t going to budge. “Okay, so now I know what a mulligan is. What the hell is a Munyon?”

“Munyon isn’t a what. He’s a who.”

“Then *who* is Munyon?”

“Munyon was a stoner kid I knew back in high school who worked at the old Golf-O-Rama in Vancouver.”

“And?” she asked.

“And if we brought him weed, or a punk bootleg or import he didn’t already have, he would let us play mini-golf for free after hours.”

“And why are we talking about him?” Trouble asked.

“Because Munyon is the one who taught me the term ‘Mulligan.’”

"Did Munyon have a first name?"

"If I ever knew it, I forgot it a long time ago. Maybe that was his first name. I feel like we're talking way more about Munyon than I'd originally planned."

Trouble paused. Her eyes narrowing before saying, "Mulligan granted."

"Thank you," I said with a slight bow. "Hi, I'm Doozer. It's so genuinely nice to meet you for the *very first time*."

"Why, yes," she replied, playing along. "Nice to meet you, Doozer. I'm Trouble."

"Say. You're that *platonic* friend of Cowboy's, aren't you?"

The sound of Trouble's laughter was as beautiful as her face.

"Why, yes, yes I am. And you're one of those little builder guys from Fraggle Rock."

"That's me." I laughed, surprised she got the reference as it flew over most bikers' heads.

"And how exactly did you come to be named after a Muppet?"

"When I first started hanging around the club, Cutter, the Saints' original president said I reminded him of the Doozers. I guess in the 80's he used to get high and watch Fraggle Rock. Anyway, I was eager. Probably too eager and was always looking for something to do. Someway to help out around the Sanctuary or the auto shop. I just love to fix stuff, ya know? Cutter started calling me Doozer before I was even a prospect and it stuck. I'm shocked you know about that show. I sure as hell didn't before Cutter."

"I grew up on an Army base and Dad's unit had a TV with a VHS player in it. We could check out VHS tapes from the base library for free, which was great, but almost all the movies were action movies from the 80's.

They only had a few tapes for kids, including Fraggle Rock which I watched the shit out of."

"So now you know how I got my name. Why do they call you Trouble?"

"Fuck around and find out," she replied with a wicked smile that made my dick hard.

"Alright. Next question then," I said. "How long have you been with your club?"

"You first," she said, finally beginning to loosen up.

"Okay, let's see," I said, doing a little math in my head. "I guess it's been six years, but I'd already become a permanent fixture around the Sanctuary by the time I started officially prospecting with the Saints."

"The sanctuary?"

"It's our clubhouse, shop, and where some of us bunk."

"How long did you prospect before you earned your patch?"

"About six months, I guess."

"Did you have to kill someone?" she asked.

"*What?*" I replied, with a nervous laugh. Her question catching me completely off guard.

"You said you wanted to have a *real* conversation, didn't you?"

"I meant a conversation without bullshit, not one that could land me in prison."

"So, you have killed someone?" Trouble asked.

"You wearing a wire?" I teased, as I thought about how much fun it would be to check her for one.

Trouble couldn't fight back a violent giggle. "The day someone gives me a badge, you know shit's about to go down."

"Seriously though. Why the questions?" I asked.

"Well, I guess I'm confused. The Saints are a one percent club, right?"

"We *were* a one percent club. Past tense," I corrected.

"What does that mean?"

"It means all club business is legal and above board and we do our best to abide by the law."

"But you haven't always been that way?"

"Back when Cutter started the Saints, there weren't many clean clubs to speak of. Nowadays, it's getting harder and harder to find an outlaw club that isn't dropping in numbers by the year. Before Cutter turned the reigns over to Minus, they figured out a way to move the club into the new millennium before we all ended up dead or in prison."

"So, you're all a bunch of Boy Scouts now?"

"You tell me? You ride with a clean club. Is every BFK member squeaky clean?"

"We're a charity organization. Every member must be sober and pass a background check."

"Wow, that's hard core. I can't say we'd all pass a background check with flying colors, but the Burning Saints are as safe as milk," I replied.

"Even milk turns bad," Trouble deadpanned.

"That's true, but so far, the straight and narrow path has been working out okay for us."

"So, you're more like a 2% club now?"

"I guess, so," I said with a laugh. "You're funny."

Trouble's cheeks pinkened as she cocked her head. "Why the change?"

"Times have changed," I replied. "Why not change with them? I like how Minus puts it. Just because the Burning Saints were born in the streets, it doesn't mean we have to die there."

"So, even though you became a member back in the day, you never had to…"

"Ice anyone? No," I replied. "Not that it's ever been

a patch requirement anyway."

"Really? I thought all one percent clubs made you get your hands wet."

"I've always been a 'left hand guy' within the club," I replied.

"What's that?"

"It means I'm the person you come to when you need something fixed."

Trouble looked me up and down but said nothing.

"Okay, enough about me," I said. "How did you and Cowboy meet?"

"I was on my way to a bike rally in Idaho—"

"Thunder Valley?"

"That's right. I was on my way to Thunder Valley and I spotted a guy in a BFK kutte broken down on the side of the road. His fuel pump quit on him just outside the state line and I stopped to see if there was anything I could do to help. The rest is history, I guess."

"You're a gearhead yourself, eh? Is that how Cowboy roped you into riding with BFK?"

"It wasn't that hard, really. After I fixed his bike, Cowboy offered to buy me lunch at a nearby diner he loved. He didn't seem like a creep and I knew of Bikers for Kids' reputation, so I said yes. Over lunch, he told me all about the club and about how they were always looking for new members. While he was talking, something clicked in my head. I was sick of being on the road alone. Tired of having no one to watch my back." She lowered her chin. "Tired of being harassed by creeps."

"How long were you a Nomad?"

"About four years," she replied.

I let out a long whistle. "Damn, that's a long time to ride solo."

"Yeah, well. Life rarely hands you options, does it?"

I could hear sadness in her voice. A vulnerability

underneath her carefully guarded exterior.

"I guess not," I replied.

"But now I've got these knuckleheads to ride with, their bikes to fix, and I get to work with the most amazing kids ever," she said, the tone of her voice suddenly turning brighter.

"It sounds like a lot of those kids have it pretty rough. It's really great what you do for them," I said.

"We do what we can. The kids are the real heroes."

Trouble was beautiful and her face lit up when she talked about the children she worked with. As she continued to tell me more about her work, I got the clear impression that her bond with them came from shared experiences. She was obviously a special person, and the more she spoke, the worse I felt about coming onto her earlier.

"Hey, I really am sorry if I was a creep earlier. I didn't mean anything by it," I said, apologetically.

"Didn't mean anything by it? So, you weren't hitting on me?" she challenged.

"No, I—"

"That's too bad," she said, this time making no attempt to hide her smile.

I stepped closer. "Too bad?"

"Yeah. Because I could use a little… ah… relief."

"Oh, yeah?"

She bit her lip, and I felt my jeans tighten behind the zipper.

"I had a thing with a guy just before we got here, and I'm still kind of spun up about it," Trouble said.

"You were with a guy before you got here?" I asked, thrown by this new bit of information.

"No, no. I wasn't *with* a guy," Trouble said, waving her hands in the air. "I had a fight with a guy. Not like a boyfriend," she corrected. "Like I punched some guy in the jaw."

"Holy shit," I chuckled. "Really?"

"Yes, and now I think I have some sort of fight or fuck instinct thing going on." She sighed. "I could use the physical distraction, if you know what I mean."

Her nervous rambling was the most adorable thing I'd ever seen, and I could not wait to devour every inch of this woman.

"Follow me." Taking her hand, I led her down the hall to an empty bunk room, locking the door behind us and crossing my arms as I watched her walk the space.

"Very biker-chic," she murmured, removing her cut, and carefully folding it before setting it on one of the bunks by the wall.

"Yeah," I agreed. "The Dogs do it right."

She smiled, toeing off her boots, then unzipping her jeans and sliding them down her hips. "You got protection?"

"Sure do," I retorted, continuing to watch her disrobe. Happily noticing the absence of a wire.

"Just so you know, I'm not a road whore. I rarely do this, but you seem kinda sweet, so—"

I smiled. "Take yes for an answer, Trouble."

Once she was in just her panties and bra, she set her boots neatly in the corner before once again folding every item with military precision and stacking them on the lower bunk.

My eyes raked over her body, taking in her cotton bikini panties and matching, white bra. Nothing lacy or girly, but sexy as fuck at the same time.

She settled her hands on her hips. "Your turn."

I grinned, removing my kutte and setting it on the chair next to one of the other bunks. The rest of my clothes, however, stayed where I dropped them.

Once I was in just boxer briefs, she stepped toward

me. “Do you mind?” she asked, pointing to my chest.

“Do whatever you want.”

She leaned in, running her tongue over the Burning Saints banner tattooed on my right pec. I was so blown away by the feeling, I let out a quiet hiss as I lifted her and dropped her gently on the lower bunk by the window, hiking her knees up and out as I pressed my face to her pussy.

She mewed quietly, sliding her fingers into my hair as I sucked her clit over the cotton of her panties. I took a second to peel them down her legs, then went right back to my task. She was already soaked, and I could smell her desire as I lapped at her folds.

Fuckin’ honey.

I slid two fingers inside of her, thrusting as I kissed my way up her body. She’d removed her bra, freeing her more than a handful tits, and I sucked a nipple into my mouth as I continued to prime her with my fingers.

“I want your dick,” she panted out and I grinned, kissing her mouth gently.

“You can have it in a second.”

I kissed her again and she bit my lip hard enough to draw blood. “I want your dick now.”

“You’re a fuckin’ tiger in the sack, huh?”

“You really don’t want to hear me roar, Doozer, so I’d get that rubber on,” she ordered, and my dick got harder.

If that was even possible at this juncture.

I knifed off the bed, removed my boxers, then grabbed a condom from my wallet, tearing the foil and rolling it on as she watched.

“I knew you’d be beautiful,” she breathed out.

I grinned, leaning over her, hovering my dick at her entrance. “You want gentle?”

“Did that bite on your lip make you think I wanted

gentle?"

I slid into her and she hissed out, "Yes," as I buried deep.

As I raised up slightly, I hit my head on the top bunk and she gasped. "Are you okay?"

I squeezed my eyes shut. "It's all good. You're not the only one who likes it hard."

Trouble let out a girly laugh. "Feel like shifting?"

"Sure." I slid out of her and gingerly stood up.

She inched off the bed, and made her way to the chair, bending down and anchoring her hands on each side, her pussy wet and ready.

I cleared my throat.

Jesus, I think I just died and went to heaven.

She glanced at me over her shoulder. "Don't let me down."

I stalked over to her, grabbing her hips as I slid into her gently.

"You good?" I asked, her pussy clenching around me.

"You talk too much," she hissed, pressing back against me.

I grinned, rocking into her, before my teasing became too much even for me, and I had to fuck her.

Hard.

I slammed into her harder and harder, deeper and deeper, and then I felt her pussy contract around my dick, and I could no longer hold back my orgasm.

I felt my balls tighten and I gripped her ass as I exploded. She did some voodoo shit with her cunt, continuing to contract her muscles, milking me dry.

"Jesus, fuck," I breathed out, sliding out of her and getting rid of the condom. I found a box of tissues and wadded a few, pressing them between her legs.

She straightened, smiling up at me. "Now, that's one

way of dealing with road fatigue."

"Yeah." I grinned, leaning down to kiss her, but she leaned back.

"You're not a cuddler, are you?"

I raised an eyebrow. "Not typically, no."

She settled her hand over my mouth before walking over to where her clothes were. "Please don't start now."

I laughed and we redressed quickly before rejoining the party.

Trouble

TWO DAYS AFTER the Dogs' party, I woke to a knock on my bedroom door. I pulled my phone off my nightstand and checked the time. It was just after ten A.M., so whoever it was just might live to see another day. Any earlier, and I couldn't be held responsible for my actions.

"You awake?" Another knock. "It's Indy."

"Come in," I groaned after making sure my ass cheeks weren't hanging outside my covers.

"Good morning," Indiana said in a tone that was far too cheery for this time of day. "There are a couple of

Saints here and one of them is askin' about you."

Indiana was in his late forties and reminded me of Taylor Kitsch, if Tim Riggins had ridden rough and smoked a lot of weed.

"What? Who?" I asked, rubbing the sleep from my eyes.

"Said his name's Doozer. You know him or should I tell him to get lost?"

"No. That's okay. I met him the other night at the Dogs' party," I said, trying to keep my tone neutral. "Tell him I'll be right out."

"Alright. I'll tell Prince Charming to warm up the glass slipper."

Indiana closed the door just in time to avoid the boot I'd hurled at his head and I heard him cackle as he walked down the hall.

All five of my housemates were guys who were older than me and they treated me like their kid sister. BFK had three houses in Portland where its members could crash. Our house had the most full-time live-in guests, followed by the place next door, which housed three guys, including Cowboy. The third house was five miles away and was used mostly for conducting club business. The rest of our members, many of whom were married, had their own places.

I dressed quickly and went to the living room to find Doozer and Sweet Pea talking with Indiana and Jimbo. As soon as he saw me, Doozer broke into a smile that sent a jolt of electricity through my stomach.

"Hey there. We didn't wake you, did we?" Doozer asked.

"It's okay. I was just about to get up anyway," I lied. This was the first day I had off in a month, and I'd planned on sleeping through most of it. Despite this, I found myself happy to see Doozer again, even if I was still a bit groggy.

"What's up? What are you doing here?" I asked.

"The Saints wanted to help spread some Christmas cheer so Minus passed the hat at last night's meeting. We came by to give Cowboy the money we collected," Doozer replied.

"That's sweet. Thank you," I said, surprised by the gesture. The Burning Saints had earned the reputation of a club you didn't want to fuck with, but Doozer had a sweetness to him that his tattoos and kutte couldn't hide.

"Yeah, well. Just trying to lend a hand," he said, before gesturing to the kitchen. "Hey, can I talk to you for a second? In private?"

I looked to see Indiana, Jimbo, and Sweet Pea all staring at us from across the room.

"Sure. Let's step outside," I said, leading us out to the front porch.

"So, you just came by to make a drop off, huh?" I asked.

"Yeah, well…" Doozer said, sheepishly. His boyish smile sending another bolt straight through me.

"Cowboy lives over there," I said, pointing to the house next door. "So whatcha doin' here?"

He laughed. "You're really gonna make me work for this, aren't you?"

I nodded.

"Alright, here it is. I haven't stopped thinking about you since the other night."

"Have you tried?" I teased.

"I can't say that I have," he said, taking a step closer. "In fact, the more I think about you, the more I want to think about you."

"Look," I said, "I don't want you to get the wrong impression about me. Like I said, I don't normally do that kind of thing and I'm not shopping for a fuck buddy or anything."

"That's good to hear, 'cause I was just gonna ask if you wanted to grab lunch with me."

"Lunch?" I said, my voice cracking.

Oh, shit. This is worse than him looking for a fuck buddy.

"Yeah," Doozer chuckled. "You know. Lunch. It's a meal some folks eat around the middle of the day. I've been on the go since five A.M. and was gonna grab a bite at Sally Anne's."

"Are you talking about a date?" I asked, unable to hide the panic in my voice.

"Well, yeah."

"I don't think that's a good idea," I said, taking a step back.

"Whoa. Wait a minute. Did I say something wrong?"

I shook my head. "It's not you. I just don't really do the whole dating thing, ya know?"

Doozer must have thought I was nuts. Less than forty-eight hours ago I was begging for him to pound me into the headboard, and now I was afraid of going to lunch with him. If he did think I was crazy, however, he wasn't letting on.

"I'm not asking for your hand in marriage, Trouble. I'm talking about sitting down over a couple of Caesar salads and a pitcher of iced tea," he said, sweetly.

"I get that," I said. "And I'm not trying to make things weird, I just think it would be best if we left what happened the other night in the past."

"The mind-blowing sex, you mean?"

"Shhhhh." I pulled Doozer away from the front door. "Yes," I whispered. "But let's not announce that to everyone in the house."

"I had a great time, didn't you?"

"Yes, but that's not the point."

"Right. The point is, you fascinate me, and I'd like to get to know you more."

This time the electricity inside my stomach was so strong it frightened me. Every one of my internal organs wanted to run away, but my skin kept them in place, frozen on my front porch.

"Doozer, you seem like a great guy, but I really think we should make this the end of the road for us. Let's just part ways here before either of us gets hurt."

"That might be a bit of a problem." Doozer's hand went to the back of his neck and his face began to flush.

"Why?"

"Earlier, when I dropped off the check, Cowboy let me know you guys were gonna be down a man on your next run."

"*And*?" I asked, terrified of what he'd say next.

"And… I sort of volunteered my services."

I took another step back. "Why the hell would you do that?"

"I told you. I want to get to know you better. I figured I could do that if—"

"If you stalked me?"

"If I was on the road with you for a few days," he corrected, stepping forward to meet me. "Honestly, I thought after the other night, you'd be into the idea."

"Well, you thought wrong," I huffed.

"Wait a minute," Doozer said, breaking into a huge smile. "You're not mad. You're chicken."

"*Chicken*? What are you? In sixth grade or something?"

"Ahhhhh," Doozer replied, waiving a finger at me. "I'm right. You're chicken."

"I'll kick your ass right here on this porch," I said.

"I don't doubt that one bit, but I'm still right," he said, folding his arms. "You had as good a time as I did the other night, and you like me."

"Immature *and* conceited," I said, unable to hide my smile.

"See? You like me, but you're too chicken to do anything about it."

"I'm not afraid of anyone," I said. "And you can take that stupid grin off your face."

"Prove it…chicken."

"I'm not chicken, I'm just not interested in you," I said.

"Bock, bock, bock," Doozer replied, folding his arms into wings, and flapping them wildly.

"Stop it," I said, my smile now turning to giggles.

"Prove it. Prove you're not chicken by letting me go on this run with you," he challenged, all the while clucking and strutting around the porch like a barnyard rooster.

It was the silliest and most endearing thing I'd ever seen a biker do, but then again, I'd never met a biker like Doozer. He was tough and clearly knew how to handle himself, but he also seemed earnest and sincere. Doozer was also right. I liked him.

"Fine, but if you step out of line, I'll pluck your feathers out one by one," I said, poking a finger in Doozer's chest.

"Wait," he said, straightening up. "*You're* supposed to be the chicken in this scenario."

"We'll see who's chicken when the first group of kids show up."

Doozer's face fell. "Kids? I thought we were just gonna make a bunch of drop offs. Cowboy didn't say anything about kids."

* * *

Doozer

We were on day three of our week-long run and so far, had already visited two youth centers, five foster homes, and three churches. Each one packed with kids. The energy needed for unloading the truck was nothing compared to what it took to keep up with them. I could see why Trouble loved working with them and admired her even more for the work she did. BFK was proving to be a great group to ride with. Cowboy and his crew rode hard, fast and kept the grumbling to a minimum. The donated truck's worrisome transmission appeared to be holding up fine and Trouble and I were getting on like a house on fire.

We gassed up our bikes and the truck, and now it was time for our band of merry elves to top off our caffeine levels. As the newbie of the group, I was elected to pick up the group's order from a coffee shop and was stoked when Trouble volunteered to go with me, as we'd had little time to ourselves. The breakneck pace of the trip coupled with the onslaught of rug rats everywhere we went made it difficult to find private time, but we stole moments whenever we could. Sometimes we'd talk, sometimes we'd make out. Either way, I looked forward to any time I could spend with her.

To my surprise, Trouble agreed to sit and have coffee with me while we waited for the group's order to be filled.

"If I didn't know any better, I'd say this looked an awful lot like one of those date things," I teased as we took our seats at the last vacant table.

"What can I say? You've caught me at a moment of un-caffeinated vulnerability." Trouble smiled.

"Trouble," the barista behind the counter of Flick's

Beanery called out.

"I've got it," I said, standing up to retrieve her order.

Trouble shot me a mock dirty look. "I can pick up my own coffee."

"I know, I know." I said, politely waving her down. "I can't help it. It's how I was raised."

Trouble's head stayed cocked defiantly to one side. She wasn't only sexy. She was devastatingly beautiful.

"If you don't let me get your coffee, my mother is gonna jump out from behind one of those potted plants and hit me with her shoe."

"That I'd like to see," she said.

"I doubt it. She'd be after you next for not allowing me to be a gentleman."

"Alright," she said, once again trying to hide her beautiful smile. "Just this once."

I went to the counter, picked up the coffee and slid a twenty to the barista while Trouble wasn't looking. The barista winked at me, no doubt hearing me and Trouble's conversation. Not that eavesdropping could be helped as Flick's wasn't much larger than a postage stamp.

"All clear?" Trouble asked as I returned to the table.

"No sign of Mama," I replied, handing Trouble her coffee. "Thanks for keeping me out of her crosshairs."

"Do you come from a big family?" Trouble asked, taking a sip.

"Not too big. We'd visit aunts, uncles, and cousins around the holidays, but growing up it was just Mama, Pop, me, and my two older sisters. And now my grandmother lives with my parents."

"Your parents are still together?"

I nodded. "Married for forty years."

"Wow, that's pretty rare these days."

"My folks are very traditional Italian," I said.

"I noticed a Virgin Mary tattoo on your chest the other night. Were you raised Catholic?"

"Mass every Sunday and sometimes Wednesday nights, too. I even did the catechism."

"What's that?" Trouble asked.

"It's something they make you do when you're a kid. You take a bunch of classes for weeks and weeks and then the priest asks you a series of questions about your faith. You know. To see if you're a good Catholic or not."

"Any of it stick?" she asked.

"I joined a one percent motorcycle club. What do you think?"

"Sure, but still…"

"What?"

"Well, there's the religious tattoos, and even though you're a biker, you're sort of…"

Trouble's cheeks flushed.

"Sort of what?" I asked.

"You know… sweet."

"Sweet? Aw, come on, man. Don't say that," I said, causing Trouble to break out in a full on smile."

"What's wrong with being sweet?" she asked.

"I'm wearing a kutte. Sweet isn't exactly the vibe I'm going for," I replied.

"Says the man with the mother of Jesus on his chest."

"In case you didn't notice, I also have tattoos of a Chinese dragon, a winged skull, and a demon wrestling an angel."

"Which one's winning?" Trouble asked.

"Maybe later you could take my shirt off and check."

Trouble cleared her throat, before asking, "Do you get along with your family?"

I chuckled. “My sisters and I have always been pretty close, and I suppose my mother and I are as well, but my relationship with my pop complicates things between us sometimes.”

“You don’t get along with your dad?”

“More like he doesn’t get along with me,” I replied. “What about you? You tight with your folks?”

Trouble shook her head. “We’re pretty…fractured.”

“I’m sorry, we don’t have to talk about—”

“It’s okay. I’m the one who brought up family,” she said.

“The other night, you said you grew up on army bases, right?”

“One base. Fort Benning in Georgia until 2008,” Trouble said, sipping her coffee. “Dad was a sniper. Kind of a bad ass actually.”

“Was he ever deployed?”

Trouble nodded. “Yeah, he served two tours in Iraq and one in Afghanistan.”

“Wow. Being apart like that must have been rough on both of you. And your mom, too.”

“Me, yes. My mom. Not so much.”

“Ouch,” I said, sensing the tension between her and her mother.

“Yeah. My mom used my dad’s deployments to relive her pre-married years, which of course meant her pre-motherhood years. She’d find some creative way to get rid of me for hours, days, and sometimes weeks while she shacked up with whatever dickhead of the month she could use and abuse, until they got sick of her, or my dad came back. Whichever came first.

“Did your dad know your mom was fucking around?”

“If he knew, he did the same thing I did, and pretended he didn’t.”

"Jesus," I ran my hand down my face. "What a fucked-up situation to pin on a kid."

"My mom wasn't what you'd call 'maternal,'" Trouble said, overemphasizing the use of air-quotes.

"Here's to family," I said, raising my coffee cup, and Trouble tipped hers to mine.

"To family," she repeated.

"You said you were only in Georgia until 2008. Then what?" I asked.

"In January of that year, my dad came back from his final deployment in Afghanistan and was given a permanent local post as an instructor at the sniper school. At first, I was ecstatic that he was home for good, but things started getting bad almost right away. He started drinking heavily and he and my mom were constantly fighting. By the end of the year, he'd been written up twice and his job was in jeopardy."

Trouble took a sip from her coffee and I noticed her hand was trembling.

"Hey, it's okay. We don't have to talk about any of this," I said, sensing her discomfort.

"No, it's okay. I never talk about my dad and for some reason I want to." Trouble's eyes met mine. "With you."

I set my cup down and took Trouble's hand.

"Was it PTSD?" I asked softly.

She nodded.

"Even though he'd done three tours he'd actually been deployed six times."

"What were the other deployments for?" I asked.

"I'm not sure. He never talked about them, but I think whatever happened between Iraq, Afghanistan, and wherever the hell else he had been, really messed him up. He was never the same after he came home. He taught me how to properly make a bed, start a fire without matches, and shoot a rifle, but never talked about what he'd seen or done while in combat," Trouble said softly, before taking a quick sip. "Anyway, he committed suicide when I was thirteen, so I never really had the chance to ask him."

"Oh, Jesus. I'm sorry," I said.

I had no idea what else to say. I had no way of relating to what she must have gone through, losing her dad at such a young age. Especially since she was so close to him and I'd spent large chunks of my childhood wishing mine would drop dead.

"It's okay. It was a long time ago," she replied, quickly wiping the tears from her eyes.

"I'm not sure there's any amount of time that would make any of what you went through okay," I said, gently squeezing her hand.

Trouble's eyes met mine. "Thanks," was all she said, but it was said with a vulnerability I'd not yet seen from her.

"Did your mom step up after your dad died?" I asked.

"Ha! Oh, god, no," she replied. "She wrecked the five-year marriage of the pervy gunnery sergeant who lived next door and married him six months after my father's funeral."

"Holy shit," I hissed.

"Then she expected me to live with this creep and act like he was my dad, and everything was normal. All the while, his old family is living directly next door. There would be shouting matches between the houses in the middle of the night. I lost count of how many times the neighbors called the M.P.s. I didn't blame them. I hated those assholes too."

"So, you split?" I asked.

"Not immediately." Trouble cocked her head, her

eyes studying me deeply for a few moments before continuing. "Jim, my so called-step dad put his hands on me, and my mother didn't do anything about it when I told her."

My blood instantly came to a boil. The mere thought of anyone hurting Trouble made me want to hurt them back. Really bad.

"I'm sorry," I said, softly, realizing that my grip on her hand had tightened reflexively, but as soon as I let go, she took my hand in hers again.

Trouble's eyes met mine again. "Stephanie," she said. "My real name's Stephanie. Cowboy started calling me Trouble the day we met, and it kind of stuck.

"I couldn't be happier to meet you, Stephanie," I said, before kissing her hand. "And you're certainly no trouble to me."

I had no idea just how wrong that statement would prove to be.

Trouble

Present Day

"REMEMBER TO CONTROL your breathing." Taxi's voice whispered in my earpiece. "Once you've lined up your shot, exhale normally, *then* hold your breath."

I pulled my eye away from the scope, trying my best to block out Taxi's chatter. I wanted to tell him to shut up and stop breaking my concentration but speaking would have meant giving up my position. Plus, the stupid jerk was right. I had a bad habit of breathing through my shots and likely would have done so if he hadn't reminded me. Of course, I'd never give him the satisfaction of telling him that.

We'd been running tactical training exercises in these damp, miserable woods all week, and although Taxi assured me I was making progress, I wasn't so sure. Taxi said he'd never seen more "raw shooting talent" in anyone before, but I wasn't so sure. Having my father as my first teacher, it was hard for me not to compare my skills to his. His shots were always clean as a whistle and I never saw him miss a target. Not even once.

"And make sure you don't driiiiift," my mentor sang softly, continuing his effort to rattle me. Not that I needed any help in that department. It had taken almost two hours of crawling on my belly through high grass to reach this spot. I was dressed in a Ghillie suit, with a fully loaded drag bag in tow. I was exhausted, cold, and most of all, nervous of missing my target.

"Oh, and Trouble. Would this be a good time to tell you that I can totally see you?" Taxi asked, smugly.

I had no idea if Taxi was telling the truth, but given that he was a decorated FBI marksman, and I'd never worn a Ghillie suit before, he likely was. For all I knew, I stuck out like a bunch of fucking broccoli. The camouflage suit only weighed five pounds, but with all its branches and covering, I felt like I'd been swallowed by a Christmas tree.

I did my best to block out Taxi's distractions and the thoughts of my father, re-lined up my shot, took a breath, and exhaled. My finger barely covering the trigger as I calculated the precise moment to fire.

Thwack.

Before I could get my shot off, a paintball exploded against my right leg.

"Mother fucker!" I screamed and I looked down to see the branches covering my burning thigh splattered with yellow paint.

I'd taken enough shots during Taxi's training exercises over the past week to know he'd fired this one from close range. Really close.

"Take your shot," Taxi said calmly.

"I've been hit," I replied.

"Are you dead or wounded?" he asked.

I sighed but didn't answer. Another paintball exploded eight inches from my head, and there was no way Taxi missed by accident. I reset for my shot, controlled my breathing, and tried my best to concentrate on my target. A plush toy cat set on top of a high tree stump. I gently squeezed the trigger, and my stomach sank as the bullet missed its mark by at least six inches. My intended target taunting me with his big stupid orange face and dumb yellow grin.

"Shit," I whispered, and awaited my punishment.

I didn't have to wait long. This time, Taxi delivered a headshot, which didn't so much hurt, due to the helmet I was wearing, but was humiliating, nonetheless. I turned my head toward the direction of the shot and could now see Taxi, dressed head to toe, in his own Ghillie suit, no more than ten yards to my right.

"How long have you been there?" I asked in utter disbelief, rising to my feet.

"Would it piss you off if I told you the entire time?" Taxi asked, grinning as he stood.

"How?"

"When you'd move, I'd move."

"So, you saw me come out of the woods?" I asked

"Saw you, heard you, smelled you."

"Shit," I said in utter defeat.

"I told you before. There's nothing I won't do to

protect President Garfield," Taxi said.

"I hate that stupid cat," I said.

"And *he* hates Mondays," Taxi replied before asking, "You know what I hate?"

"What?" I asked begrudgingly.

"Dead team members," he replied.

My eyes darted to the ground.

"Look at me, Trouble." Taxi said, firmly. "You are more than capable of making this shot, but you were spun up. Your technique is improving, but you're still inside your head."

"I know," I said.

"Acknowledging your weaknesses isn't enough. Controlling your breathing isn't enough either. You have to be able to control your emotions in the field or you are going to miss your target, or worse..."

"Oncoming enemy forces," I said.

"They're always out there, and you'll never see them coming unless your head is on a swivel at all times. You got that?"

"Roger," I replied.

"Good. Let's go get some chow. Keeping the president safe has made me hungry for lasagna," Taxi said, pointing to the plush cat, who's suction cup paws reached out toward us.

"I can't," I replied. "There's a big club party at the Sanctuary today and I kinda have to be there."

"Oh, that's right. Cricket invited me but I'm packing up the last of my things and turning the keys over to the landlord this afternoon so I'm afraid I'll have to miss the festivities."

"That's too bad. It's gonna be a packed house," I said, before asking, "What does Garfunkle the cat have to do with eating lasagna?" causing Taxi to stare at me blankly.

“Gar*funkle* is a folk singer.” Taxi pointed to the stuffed animal in the distance. “That beloved cat’s name is Gar*field.* He hates Mondays and loves lasagna. How do you not know this?

I shrugged.

“What kind of childhood did you have?” he asked in disbelief.

“Can’t tell ya’,” I replied.

“I’d hoped by now, you could tell me anything, Trouble,” Taxi said, softly.

I chuckled nervously. “No, I mean, I can’t tell you, because I never had one.”

Taxi studied me silently, before saying, “Doctor Fenton is going to have a field day with you,” before turning and heading out of the brush.

“Who’s Doctor Fenton?” I asked, walking almost double-time in order to keep up with Taxi’s pace, my drag bag feeling at least five pounds heavier than it did this morning.

“She’s the chief psychologist at Quantico. She’s the one that will oversee your psych eval.”

“*If* I agree to go,” I said, already running out of breath.

“You’ll also have to beef up your cardio,” Taxi said.

“*If* I agree to go,” I repeated.

Taxi spun around and stopped dead in his tracks, causing me to run into him, damn near bouncing off his chest.

“I get on a plane for Virginia in two days, Trouble. You need to decide right now if you’re going to be on the seat next to me or not.”

“I told you not to pressure me.”

“Pressure you? I’ve been nothing but patient with you, but we’re out of time.”

“How can I leave Portland now? How could I even

think about leaving the club after all they've done for me, and after everything that's gone down over the past year?"

"You mean, how could you leave Doozer?" Taxi replied.

My eyes darted to the ground, but Taxi's stern, but caring voice pulled my focus back to him.

"Trouble. You need to figure out what's best for you and your future. This is a once in a lifetime opportunity that you're being given, and I strongly suggest you take hold of it."

"Easy for you to say. You don't have anything to lose," I said.

"Hey," Taxi snapped. "I'm putting my ass on the line for you. You're the youngest, and by far the least experienced, person I'm recommending for this team. And if this team fails, I can pretty much kiss my career with the FBI goodbye. Not to mention all the good we're trying to do."

"I'm sorry, I didn't mean—"

"Button that lip," Taxi growled. "How the hell do you think I'm gonna look to my new boss, when the cadet candidate I recommended doesn't show up for her entrance interview?"

"Taxi, I'm not trying to—"

Thwack.

Another spray of yellow followed by another sting. This time on top of my right foot.

"Would you please stop shooting me?" I yelled.

"I need an answer," was all Taxi said.

"Minus isn't gonna be happy."

"You let me deal with Minus," Taxi said.

I bit my lip. "Doozer is *not* going to take this well."

"He'll understand," Taxi said.

I cocked my head and raised an eyebrow.

"Okay, he's gonna lose his shit, but if he cares about you, he'll support your decision."

Taxi was right and I didn't know which idea scared me more. The possibility of Doozer being angry about me going to Virginia, or of him being supportive. If he were gung-ho about the idea, I'd have one less excuse for staying. But there was one more possibility.

"What if he doesn't care at all that I'm leaving?" I asked softly.

"Something tells me, that's not going to be the case." Taxi replied.

* * *

Doozer

"The left side is still too low. Raise it up about three inches," I called up to Tacky, co-member of the newly assembled Burning Saints decorating committee. He was balanced at the very top of a ten-foot aluminum, A-frame ladder. His boots covered the red and black safety sticker which read, "WARNING: DO NOT USE AS A STEP."

"How about that?" he asked after adjusting the wrong side.

"No, your *other* left, dumbass." I yelled.

"You wanna climb up here and hang this fuckin' thing?" Tacky asked.

"No way," I replied. "This is our tallest ladder and you're the only one stupid enough to stand at the top of it. Besides, only your freak monkey arms can reach the rest of the way."

"Anyone ever tell you you're a mean fucker first thing in the morning?" Tacky asked, raising up the sign which read, "CONGRATULATIONS CHAMP."

Clutch, our club's Sergeant at Arms, and his wife, Eldie, had recently adopted two kids they'd taken in off the streets. Alejandro, who we all called "The Kid," was a scrappy seventeen-year old who Clutch almost murdered the first night they met.

The Kid had stolen and trashed Clutch's beloved 1971 Barracuda, Lucille, as his initiation into a rival club of ours called Los Psychos. We eventually made peace with Los Psychos, and it didn't take too long for Clutch to take a shine to the kid. They bonded quickly over boxing and eventually began to repair Lucille together. Shortly after taking Alejandro in, Clutch and a very pregnant Eldie began fostering his eight-year-old sister, Celia. Callie, Sweet Pea's old lady, is a lawyer and helped big time with their adoption process. Through her connections and expertise in family law, she was able to cut through years of red tape.

Alejandro was proving to be a boxing phenom, winning his first three amateur bouts, two by way of knock out. Making his father and trainer, Clutch, the happiest member of our club. His most recent victory was for the local Golden Gloves title which meant he could now qualify to compete at the state level.

"Right there. That's better," I said once the sign was level.

"That's exactly where I had it the first time!" Tacky argued.

"Keep on giving me shit and I'll kick this ladder out from underneath you. I think Sweet Pea's old wheelchair is still around here somewhere," I said.

"Mean *and* in a shitty mood," he said, climbing down. "Come on, man. Decorating ain't so bad. It could be worse. Cricket has Spike power-washing the driveway right now."

Tacky wasn't entirely wrong about my mood, although, it had nothing to do with decorating or with the early hour. It had everything to do with the fact that I'd woken up alone. Again.

Since Trouble and I started bunking together six months ago, mornings had become the best part of my day. Especially when she'd get up first. Trouble was horniest in the morning and there was nothing better than being woken up by her ass grinding on my cock. But there had been no grinding this morning, or yesterday, or the two days before that. In fact, I'd barely seen her all week, let alone spent any amount of quality time with her.

Quality time? Jesus in a Chrysler, I sound like a fucking chick.

"There, I told you it was straight," Tacky said, backhanding my chest as he admired his handywork.

"Come on, let's go see what the queen requires next," I said, and we headed for the kitchen.

The Sanctuary was packed to the rafters. Minus had made it crystal fucking clear that this party was a mandatory event. All Saints on deck. Officers and senior club members were already cracking beers and jokes while us younger soldiers and prospects kept ourselves busy.

The kitchen was in a state of what you might call 'controlled chaos.' Cricket, Minus's old lady and club den mother, was busy calling out instructions to her team of apprentice chefs… a group of Saints, dressed in leather, denim, and white aprons.

"Socks, please check on that last batch of cupcakes, sweetie. I need to know the moment they are cool enough for Hacksaw to start frosting them."

"Sure thing, boss lady," Socks replied affectionately.

When Cutter appointed Minus as club president, he also asked Cricket to join him. His idea was for her to act as a sort of business manager for the club. Minus and Cricket were to work hand-in-hand to secure the club's future. Cutter's plan worked out better than he could have imagined. Minus and Cricket were rock-solid partners, and the club was flush with cash even though we'd ended all street-level business almost three years ago. Minus had already been tested several times by outside clubs since his appointment and had proved to be a great wartime president and leader. The club also loved Cricket and I didn't know a single member that wouldn't take a bullet in the face for her. Still, I couldn't help but laugh at the sight of bikers in aprons. As much as Cutter wanted the club to clean up our act before we all ended up in jail or dead, I'm sure even he could never have envisioned Burning Saints frosting cupcakes in the Sanctuary kitchen.

"How's the sign looking, boys?" an extremely focused Cricket asked, while vigorously stirring the contents of a large metal bowl.

"Just like Warthog," I said.

"How's that?" Cricket asked, without looking up.

"Straight and high," I replied, stealing a freshly baked cookie from a nearby tray.

"I saw that," Cricket scolded without ever looking up from her bowl.

"Damn, boss lady. Your kids aren't gonna get away with shit."

"*Kids?* I think I've got my hands full with just the one for now," she replied with a chuckle.

"This is true."

Minus and Cricket's son, Cutter Randall 'Little Cut' Vincent, was not quite one year old and already hell on wheels…in a good way.

"Things might slip a little when we have more," Cricket continued. "Of course, we should probably get on that, huh? Minus and I are already three behind Clutch and Eldie."

Besides their two newly adopted children, Clutch and Eldie were also proud parents of twin daughters, who'd spent their first precious moments of life in the neonatal intensive care unit at OHSU. The babies were born prematurely, which I guess is common for twins, but the girls arrived six weeks early, and things were pretty touch and go for a while.

I laughed and asked, "Anything else you need me and Tacky to take care of?"

Before Cricket could answer, the kitchen's back door swung open and Kitty walked in, his frame, blocking the entire doorway. "Hey, little man," he said. "You got a minute?"

"Yeah," I said, and followed him back to his makeshift office.

"Remember that judge you asked me to look into?"

"Yeah."

"Got a flag."

I'd had him investigate Judge Snodgrass over a year ago, and even though nothing linking the judge with my father had come up initially, Kitty had assured me he'd keep digging. If there was any kind of connection between my father and the Judge, he'd find it.

"What did you find?" I asked and he handed me a sheet of paper.

"It's a business license for the Mayflower Development Corporation that was filed back in January," he replied.

"What's the Mayflower Development Corporation?"

"From what I've been able to find, they are a residential housing developer," Kitty said.

"What's so interesting about that?"

"Look at who applied for the license," he instructed.

I scanned the paper and found the name. "Patricia Snodgrass?"

"The judge's daughter," Kitty said.

"Okay? So, judge Snotty's daughter is into real estate. So what?"

"Here's what," Kitty said, grinning proudly before handing me another piece of paper.

"What is this?"

"It's a 2702-B tax form, courtesy of the Internal Revenue Service."

"Do I want to know how this document came into your possession?"

"No, you do not, little man. Besides, the important thing isn't how I got it, but what's on it. Check out who's listed as the owner of the Mayflower Development Corporation."

"Who's Leo Vox?"

"Not who, but what," Kitty said. "Leo Vox is a shell corporation owned by a single person."

"Who?"

"Berto Mancini," Kitty said.

"My father?" My heart sank. "What the hell is my father doing setting up a shell corporation, and what does it all have to do with Judge Snotty and his daughter?"

"This is all I have for now, but I'm gonna keep digging. If there's anything interesting to find, I'll fuckin' find it."

"Thanks, Kitty," I said.

"Any time, little man," he replied and walked away.

I walked back to the kitchen, my head spinning, just as Trouble entered, looking like a soggy pile of leaves. Her camouflage suit was soaking wet and riddled with bright yellow paint splotches. She was shivering and looked completely miserable.

"Holy shit, it's Swamp Thing!" I cried out.

Trouble ignored my comment and turned to Cricket.

"Sorry about your kitchen, I'll clean up the mess."

"It's okay, sweetie. It's just a little water," Cricket replied.

"Not that mess," Trouble said dryly, before firing a paintball directly to my mid-section.

Doozer

"OW! THAT SHIT stings!" I cried out to the delight of Cricket's kitchen staff.

"Serves you right for calling her a swamp creature," Cricket scolded.

"I said Swamp Thing. You know. The comic book," I corrected.

"That's the problem. Guys know too much about comic books, and not enough about how to treat women."

"Oh, yeah," I challenged. "How's that?"

"You should treat her like a princess," Cricket said.

Trouble and I looked at each other and burst out laughing.

"Thank you for having my back, Cricket, but I'm afraid this turd bucket is right. None of that princess crap for me. I'd never be caught dead in a ball gown. Besides, he's usually extremely sweet to me. Not that he'd dare show it in front of all you macho assholes."

More laughs from our apron-clad brothers filled the kitchen.

Trouble patched over to the Burning Saints from BFK about a year ago and had no problems fitting right in with our crew. We needed another capable mechanic, and Cowboy felt she was ready for a change. "Hungry to chew on somethin' new for a while," as he put it. She'd grown up riding and proven herself to be loyal to both BFK and the Saints. She was tough, smart, a more than capable mechanic, and the sexiest woman I'd ever crossed paths with.

I leaned in a gave her a kiss. "I don't care if the whole world knows. I'll shout it from the rooftop," I said, cupping my hands around my mouth. "I'm in love with a shrub!"

Trouble began to raise her rifle, but I stopped her with another kiss.

"That's better," she said softly.

Growing up, I'd been taught to keep expectations of people low. My father constantly drilled into me that people were mostly selfish and never to be trusted. He told me repeatedly to never base my future on anyone else. The sooner I got used to the idea that I was on my own, the better, but for the first time in my life I was looking forward to my future. A future with her.

"How 'bout we get you out of these wet clothes and

into a hot shower?" I asked.

"Even better still," she replied.

"I'm gonna take Trouble to our bunk. I'll be back in a bit." I told Cricket and led my woman back to our shared space. I'd never lived with any of my girlfriends before and I was surprised by how great it was. At least it was great with her. I'm not sure how I would feel with someone else, but with her, things were pretty easy fuckin' breezy.

Until recently, that is.

Trouble stripped her gear off and I started the shower. The bunk houses were among the oldest buildings on the Sanctuary property and the water took forever to heat up. If things with Trouble kept going well, I was hoping to find us an apartment of our own in Portland. Even though Trouble had a "tom-boy" streak and could hang with the guys, she was still one hundred percent woman. Tough, but sensitive. Sometimes I had to remind myself not to take my teasing too far. She was an only child who'd lost her father when she was young. I was used to sibling rivalries, competition, and endless ball breaking.

"Hey, you okay?" I asked, sensing something was on her mind. "I didn't actually hurt your feelings with that swamp thing shit, did I?"

"What?" She replied, clearly lost in thought. "No, no. It's nothing. We can talk about it later."

"Well, which is it?" I asked. "Nothing, or is there something we need to talk about?"

She smiled. "Honestly, talking is the last thing I want to do right now."

"Oh, yeah? What do you want to do?"

"How 'bout you strip and join me in the shower, and I'll show you."

She didn't have to ask twice.

* * *

Trouble

I stepped into the shower and shoved my head under the hot water. God, what the hell was I going to say to Doozer? Luckily, he was a man who never turned down sex and every time I needed to distract him, I just showed him my tits. It worked every time and often helped to distract me as well.

Just like clockwork, Doozer joined me in the shower, already hard and ready, turning me to face him and kissing me like it would be our last.

And maybe it would be.

I forced back tears, sliding my tongue across his as he lifted me and braced my back against the tile, burying his beautiful cock to the hilt. I gripped his shoulders and arched as much as I could in the tiny space.

"Fuck," he breathed out. "So good."

"I need more," I begged, and he slid out, stepping back so I could settle my feet on the floor.

"Ankles," he ordered, and I bent down and grabbed my ankles.

The second he'd discovered I'd had ten years of gymnastics as a kid and was more flexible than the average human, this position had become one of his favorites.

My body was primed, my nipples were hard, my pussy soaked, and I needed him inside of me. Luckily, I didn't have to wait long, and he held me steady as he slid into me from behind.

"You good?" he grunted out.

"Yes," I rasped.

"Trust me?"

"Fuck, yeah."

He made sure I was secure and wouldn't slip, then

he reared back and slammed so deep, I cried out as I almost came.

"Towel rail," he bit out and I raised enough to grip the rail, then he was slamming so hard, I came twice before he was close to done. But then his finger slid into my tight hole and I exploded again.

"Marco!" I screamed, and he wrapped his arms around me, lifting me, my back to his front as his cock pulsed inside of me.

"We're not done," he growled, letting me clean up before turning off the water and carrying me to the bed, despite the fact we were both soaking wet.

Settling me gently on the mattress, he pushed my knees apart and kissed the inside of one thigh, then the other before running his tongue along my folds, sucking my clit gently as he slid two fingers inside of me.

I gripped his scalp and slid one leg over his shoulder, while I dug my other heel into the bed, lifting my hips slightly to get closer.

As I rode the wave to another orgasm, he kissed his way up my body, drawing a nipple into his mouth as his cock pressed at my entrance.

"Marco," I begged, and he slid his tip inside of me, grinning as he ran his tongue over my lips.

"What do you want, Steph?"

I don't want to leave you.

"I want your dick to tear my pussy apart."

"Happily," he breathed out, slamming into me, linking my fingers with his and dragging them above my head, holding them hostage with one hand as he slid the other between our bodies and worked my clit.

I tried to pull my hands away, but he was too strong, so I wrapped my legs around his waist and met every thrust with one of my own.

It was too much.

He let out a quiet grunt, then he released my hands, continuing to work my clit with one hand while rolling a nipple with the other.

My orgasm rolled over me slow and sweet as he covered my mouth with his and kissed me gently.

I grinned against his lips. "It's always so, so good," I panted out.

"I love you, baby."

"Love you too."

"Time to tell me what's been buggin' you," he announced, sliding out of me, and rolling onto his back. He tugged me over his chest and patted my bottom. "All of it."

"We have to get back to the party," I said, hoping to avoid the conversation for as long as possible. Even though I knew we had to have it. "Cricket looked like she needed all the help she could get."

"Nice try, blue eyes," Doozer said, with a squeeze. "Come on. Spill."

"Okay," I sighed. "You know Taxi, right?" Starting off on the clumsiest of conversation foot possible?"

"Taxi? The FBI agent who saved both our lives? Yeah, I think I'm familiar," Doozer teased.

Last year a rival club called the Gresham Spiders planned to kidnap and execute a member of the Burning Saints and Doozer had been selected. Wolf, their new chapter president, was looking to settle a score with Minus, and wanted to send our club a clear message that the Spiders were not to be fucked with. Taxi was working undercover as a member of the Spiders and intervened, saving Doozer's life. He also stepped in when I went after Wolf with my father's gun. I didn't know Doozer was alive at the time, and had Taxi not stopped me, I wouldn't be.

"Stop it," I said, playfully smacking his bare, rock-hard, chest. "This is hard for me."

"Okay, I'm sorry, babe," he said, clearing his throat. "I'm listening."

"Well, you know we've been working together every day on my shooting—"

"Oh shit."

Doozer sat up suddenly, taking me along for the ride.

"Are you gonna tell me that you and Taxi are fucking?" he asked, in a way that sounded more hurt than accusatory.

"What? Ew. Gross. No, you idiot," I squealed and smacked his chest again, this time not so playfully. "He's offered me a position on a team he's putting together."

"A team? What does that mean?"

"It means Taxi wants me to come work for him at the FBI as a tactical shooter."

"Work for him… as in… like a job?"

"That's the idea," I replied.

Doozer broke into a wide smile. "That's fuckin' fantastic, baby! I'm so proud of you."

"You're not upset?"

"Upset? Hell, no. This is great news," Doozer said excitedly. "Besides, a second ago I thought you were gonna leave me for Taxi."

"Why do you always think I'm looking to shack up with an older man?"

"Maybe it's because I still can't believe you waste your time with a biker bum like me," he replied.

"You are not a bum," I scolded, before kissing his soft, full lips.

"Try telling that to my dad," Doozer said.

"You could tell him yourself if you ever talked to him."

"We talk," Doozer replied, dismissively.

"You talked for a minute and a half on the phone over a month ago, and that was about RV parts."

"Yeah. Like I said. We talk."

"Did you really think I was hooking up with Taxi?"

"No, not really. It's not like I don't trust you or anything like that. It's just that the two of you have been spending a lot of time together and we haven't. You know. It makes a guy wonder. That's all."

"Doozer," I said with an exaggerated gasp. "Are you jealous?"

"Jealous? Me? No way."

"Mmmm hmmm."

"Look at it from my perspective. Here you are, the sexiest, most beautiful woman in the world, and you're out in the woods, alone with some dude."

"Some dude? A second ago, you brought up the fact that Taxi saved your life."

"*Our* lives," Doozer corrected. "Plus. He *did* sort of kill me."

"First of all, it's still too soon to joke about the time we all thought you were dead, and secondly he didn't save my life, he prevented me from ending Wolf's."

"Which would have gotten you killed by the Spiders for sure," he said.

"You don't know that" I said, knowing full well Doozer was right.

"What I do know for sure is that I'm glad Taxi was there that night to stop you. I also know how incredible you are, and I'm not surprised he wants to hire you."

"Thank you," I said, kissing him again. "I'm so glad you didn't freak out. I was really worried you were going to be upset about all of this."

"How could I be anything but happy for you? Besides, it means all these mornings without you were worth it. Your training obviously went well, and once you know your schedule, we can finally synch back up. Plus, now that you're working, that'll speed up our plans to move out of the Sanctuary and get our own place."

My heart sank like stone and my face must have shown it.

"What is it?" Doozer asked.

"My training isn't over just yet," I replied. "It's only just starting, and…"

"And?"

"And the FBI doesn't have a training facility in Portland."

"So, what? You keep running around in the woods with Taxi until you're officially hired? For how long?"

"Not exactly," I said. "Taxi is taking me back with him to Quantico, Virginia, where he'll report for his new post, and I'll begin training at the FBI training academy."

"Quantico?" Doozer asked in a tone and manner more akin to what I had originally expected. "For how long?"

"Eight weeks."

"That's two fucking months," he growled.

"Normally, training at Quantico is twenty weeks, but Taxi's team is being fast-tracked. Some of the other guys have already started." I said, hoping these bits of information would alleviate the sting of the news.

"Oh, that solves everything," he replied.

"I thought you were happy for me?"

"I was…I am, I… just thought you meant Taxi was offering you a job here in Portland, not on the other side of the fucking country. Not that you would be gone for two fucking months."

I broke eye contact and said nothing.

"Trouble? There's something else you're not telling

me. What is it?"

Dammit.

"Once training is over, I may not be coming back to Portland at all."

Doozer

"SO, YOU'RE KICKING my ass to the curb after all," I said, shooting out of bed.

"No, it's just that the team Taxi's putting together may not be based out of Portland. It sounds like it might not be based out of *anywhere*."

"What the fuck is that supposed to mean?"

"I don't know. I'm not sure, and there's not a whole lot I can tell you, other than I'm not breaking up with you."

"You're moving to Virginia for two months and who

the hell knows where after that, and this is the first I'm hearing of it?" I dragged my hands down my face. "Not really interested in the long-distance thing, ya know."

"Oh, that's great," Trouble hissed. "My pussy won't be at your beck and call, so now you're dumping *me*?"

"I'm not the one skulking around in the dark hours of the morning with another man."

"There's no fucking skulking, Marco. I have given you my schedule from the get," she growled. "If you'll notice, I gave you so much detail, even down to when I may or may not need to pee."

I sighed. I was being a complete asshole, but I couldn't seem to control the emotions swamping me.

"Train here," I rasped.

"I can't."

"Why the fuck not?" I bellowed.

"Because that's not how this works!" she bellowed back. "And now I'm wondering if you've always been a dick or if it's just me who brings it out in you."

"Goddammit!" I snapped, my fist connecting with the wall, punching a perfect circle in the drywall as permanent reminder of my blind stupid rage.

"Doozer," she admonished, sliding off the mattress and approaching me like she might a feral cat ready to attack her. "Let's back this up a little," she said, placing her hands tentatively on my chest. "Take a breath."

I squeezed my eyes shut and did just that.

"Now take another," she directed, and I met her eyes. "I'm not leaving you."

"Bullshit."

She gripped my chin and squeezed. "I'm not fucking leaving you, Doozer. You are one of the most important things in my life, but I'm also well aware that if I give up a dream for a boy, then I'm a douche, and I will never, *never* be a douche, capiche?"

I pulled my face out of her vice grip and dropped my forehead to hers. "Jesus, Steph, you're not a douche."

"I know." She cupped my face again, this time gently, and she ran her thumb over my lower lip. "If I could take you with me, I would. The thought of being away from your magic wand, even for a night, makes me crazy, but this is important to me. It's a chance at a purpose, honey. One that I'd very much like to share with you."

"And if you decide I'm not part of that purpose?" I whispered, my gut churning with every fear spoken aloud.

"How could you not be part of my purpose, Marco? You're the reason any of this is even happening."

"And if that reason is bigger than us? What if we drown?"

"There are lots of things that will be bigger than us, honey. And we won't drown. We're fucking champion swimmers."

She grinned and I couldn't stop a smile myself.

"You're better at the backstroke than I am," I retorted.

She pushed on my chest, backing me to the bed. "Then I think you need to practice." She shoved me and I fell onto the mattress, and she promptly straddled me.

Trouble

"ABSOLUTELY, FUCKING, ABSOLUTELY, not," Minus bellowed. His huge hand slapping down on the top of his heavy oak desk.

"You said absolutely twice," I replied, dryly.

"That's how fucking absolute I am."

"Minus—"

He shook his head. "This isn't gonna happen."

"Can you please just hear us out?"

"No fucking way, Trouble. BFK may play fast and

loose about its members coming and going but the Burning Saints don't. I told you that when you patched over. The Saints are a full-time club."

"I'm not asking for vacation time, Minus. Taxi is asking for my help. He's asking me to be part of something important."

"So, the Saints aren't important to you? The work you do with us for our community isn't important?"

"No, of course not. That's not what I meant."

"Look, Trouble. When Cowboy and I talked about you coming to our club he told me that you'd need to stay busy. He said, as long as you had something to do with your hands, the ghosts in your head would stay quiet. He also warned me that you had a good streak of wanderlust in you. Between your shop schedule and the volunteer work you do with Cricket, I figured we had the first part licked. And I can send you on a run any time you like if you need to get some road under your tires."

"Minus, this is about something more important than road trips and community fundraisers," Taxi said.

"You must have moose balls to come into my office and tell me you're gonna take one of my patches."

Taxi raised his hands. "I never said I was taking—"

"We had a deal, and now you just waltz in here and try to claim Trouble as property of the US government."

"Wait a minute. I am no one's fucking property," I said, shooting to my feet. "Not yours or his."

"You sit the hell down." Minus pointed angrily at me.

"Don't get pissed at her," Taxi protested.

"You shut the fuck up," Minus yelled.

"Look, Minus." Taxi rose to his feet. "I respect you and all—"

"Would you two please knock it off?" I said, to no

avail.

"Goddammit, stop fucking interrupting me," Taxi shouted.

"Get the fuck out of my office," Minus shouted even louder.

And so it continued. Minus screaming at Taxi, and vice versa, while I tried and failed to get a word in. Until I couldn't stand it any longer. Men had dictated my future one way or another for most of my life and I'd simply had enough.

"Shut the hell up!" I screamed at the top of my lungs. "Both of you. This is my life, and I can do whatever the hell I want with it." I turned to Minus. "I'm your patch not your possession. If you want to kick me out of the club for insubordination, I'll heat up the brand myself, but I'm not leaving otherwise. I knew what I was doing when I patched in and my loyalty to the Burning Saints has never wavered. The whole reason Taxi wants me to be part of his team is because I'm a biker. I'm not asking to leave, just a chance to broaden my horizons while helping to protect the club the best way I can."

"Alright, alright. I can hear you fine. Let's all take it down a notch," Minus said, returning to his seat. Taxi and I followed suit.

"The Beast is getting stronger, Minus," Taxi said. "Daphne might be in the wind, but she's clearly still calling the shots in Savannah. Los Psychos are fully under their thumb and our intel says the Spiders are next. The Beast organization is smart, well-funded, and ruthless. They're poised to infiltrate and influence every major player in the southern US, and they will continue moving west if we don't stop them. The FBI needs a foothold into their world, and I'm risking my career by betting on bikers to get the job done. Training has already started in Virginia and I'm out of time."

"If the Beast poses such a big threat, why does this team of yours consist of bikers and hackers? Why doesn't the FBI put together a proper task force?" Minus asked.

"I'm in charge because I helped put Wolf in prison, which made my boss look good to the top brass. You helped me, which earned your sweetheart deal with the FBI, and a promise to help bring the Beast down," Taxi replied.

"That deal never said anything about using our members as bait."

"She's not gonna be bait," Taxi said. "She's going to be a trained operative, working under my command. You already know what a good shot she is with a long gun. Probably the best raw talent I've ever seen, but she could be great if I had more time with her."

"Great at killing people," Minus ground out, and I heard something in his tone that I hadn't before. A layer of sorrow.

"Great at protecting her team from a safe vantage point," Taxi countered.

"I can see what you get out of the deal, but what about Trouble? What about the Saints?" Minus asked.

"The best thing Trouble can do for the Burning Saints is to help me stop the Beast," Taxi replied.

"And Trouble can decide what's best for Trouble," I said.

"That would be true if not for that," Minus said, pointing to my kutte.

He was right and I knew it. I swore an oath on Red Dog's staff when I joined the Saints. I'd committed myself to the club and the authority of its president. Minus had every right to keep me in Portland and I wasn't surprised he was pissed at Taxi for "poaching" one of his members. As club president, Minus felt responsible for me, and I truly cherished that, but I really needed him to understand how important this was to me.

"What did your road captain have to say about all of this?" Minus asked.

"I haven't said anything to Sweet Pea, yet. I thought it would be best to speak to you first."

"And what about Doozer?

"He supports me," I said.

Minus chuckled. "Uh, huh."

"What's that supposed to mean?" I challenged.

"It means for a couple of sharp-shooters, neither of you are very sharp."

"What?"

"Neither of you have a clue what a thorn in your fuckin' side that kid is gonna be the moment Trouble's plane is wheels up."

"I've already had a talk with him, and he's fine with me going," I countered. "We know it'll be hard, but—"

"You don't know shit," Minus interrupted. "That boy is over the fuckin' moon for you, and if you leave his orbit, gravity is gonna fuck with his head, big time."

"Minus—"

"No," he said. "Abso-fucking-lutely not. End of conversation. Now, get the fuck out of my office."

* * *

Minus

"Is that really what you said?" Cricket asked me after I'd filled her in on my conversation with Taxi and Trouble.

I was currently sitting on our bed, my back against the headboard, watching my wife undress. Slowly. I had a feeling she was angling for something.

I just wasn't sure what… yet.

"Yeah, what else *could* I say?"

She raised an eyebrow. "Oh, I don't know… yes?"

"Fuck, no," I countered. "She's my first female patch, she's fuckin' awesome, and I've never in my life known a better mechanic."

"Except Hatch."

Hatch was Cricket's brother and the president of the Dogs of Fire in Portland.

"She's better than Elwood. Better than Doozer, and even better than Hatch."

Cricket raised an eyebrow, unbuttoning her silk blouse. "Bullshit."

I licked my lips as she slid her top off, throwing it into the dry-cleaning pile. She settled her hands on her hips, giving me full view of her lacy bra, and I was instantly hard. It didn't help that she was still in her pencil skirt and strappy heels.

"She's *as* good," I corrected. I had to walk a fine line with Cricket and her relationship with her brother. He was one of the reasons I was exiled to Savannah back when my love affair with her was getting hot and heavy.

Hatch didn't feel I was good enough for her, so for me, he was the man who'd kept me from the only woman I've ever loved.

For Cricket, however, he was not only her brother, but the man who'd stepped up when their mother died, and their father went to prison. Hatch had been barely a man himself when he took on the responsibility of his younger siblings, making sure none of them were separated. He'd raised them the best he knew how and although she knew he wasn't perfect, he was certainly her hero.

Her first.

So, even though I knew beyond a shadow of a doubt she would pick me over him any day, it would devastate her if either of us made her do that. So Hatch and I'd come to a level of a courteous truce, and our clubs were friendly, which gave us both backup we'd found we'd needed over the past few years.

She gave me a slight smile. "Okay, as good."

I waved a finger toward her. "Keep going, baby. I'm liking the strip tease."

She rolled her eyes and removed her watch and rings, setting them in her jewelry box, then facing me again. "Why did you say 'no,' honey? The real reason?"

Jesus, the woman could get to the heart of a matter within seconds. "That *is* the real reason?"

"Jase," she said, her tone one of admonishment.

"Right here, baby."

"Dig deep." She crossed her arms, pushing her glorious tits up higher. Ever since giving birth and breastfeeding, her tits were larger than normal, and she was stacked to begin with. "You know Taxi's recruiting. You know he's pulling from the Dogs and the Howlers, as well as from us, and you know we could live without her for a little while. Give me the real reason."

I palmed my eye sockets in an effort to ward off a headache. "If she goes, Doozer's gonna be a complete waste of fuckin' space."

"Aw," she cooed. "You big ol' softy."

"Don't you dare," I warned, and she chuckled, sliding her skirt down her thighs, but keeping her shoes on.

Fuck me, she was delicious.

"I just remember how fucked up I was when I went to Savannah," I explained.

"But it was good for you in the end."

"Was it?" I challenged. "Cutter wanted to toughen me up. Focus me. And it made me hard, but did it make me too hard?"

She glanced at my growing erection and nodded.

I chuckled. "He's gone for her, baby. I know that feeling. I remember feeling that level of love as a younger man, and not having you close fuckin' gutted me."

Cricket shrugged. "Then send him with her."

"And lose *two* patches?" I snapped. "No fuckin' way."

"You've just said that if she goes, he'll be useless, so fix that."

"I have. She's not going."

"But she wants to go."

"So?" I growled. "She knew what she was doing when she patched-in."

"She was in love," Cricket said. "She patched-in to stay with Doozer."

"She patched-in because Doozer and Elwood were so busy with custom bike orders, I needed another mechanic, and this is the best club in the U.S. of fuckin' A."

"This is all very true," she conceded. "But…"

"But?

"You don't think Trouble has the right to pick which path in life she takes?" Cricket asked. "That young woman has had her life dictated to her from the get-go and she's spinning out of control, honey. And you know I know what that's like."

"She's not spinning out of control."

Cricket leaned toward me. "She's absolutely spinning. She's just really fucking good at hiding her emotions. And you know it."

I sighed. She was right. I did know it. Trouble was on edge. She was itching for something, but I'd talked myself into believing she was just itching to ride. We'd been shuttered at the Sanctuary due to Portland rain and we were all jonesing for the road.

"The problem is, if she goes to Quantico, Doozer's gonna lose his fuckin' mind whether he's here *or* there. He's dealing with all this shit with his dad, and he's also got some major anger issues he's gotta get hold of. If he fucks up on FBI turf, it could mean jail time."

She pulled the clip out of her hair and her blonde waves fell gently around her shoulders. "Then that's on him, honey."

"It's not on him, Christina, it's on me." I slapped my chest. "It means I'm not doin' my job and protectin' him."

She sighed. "The ultimate protection is letting him love his woman. Taxi will be there to monitor any issues that come up, and Duke and Pearl are barely eight hours away by car. If things get hairy, you can call the cavalry."

Duke was the man who'd healed me. He owned a ranch in the Georgia countryside, and he'd ridden with the Burning Saints back in the seventies. He'd never patched into the Burning Saints, but the club had adopted him, anyway. He'd been married to his woman, Pearl, for more than fifty years and he was still a badass at almost eighty.

"I can't subject Duke and Pearl to Doozer. They're elderly, and it's too much."

Cricket settled her knee on the bed, hoisting herself onto the mattress and straddling me. "You're so cute when you're being ridiculous. Duke could still kick *your* ass."

I cupped her breasts, tugging the cups down to free her nipples, running my tongue over one nipple, then the other.

"Was this your plan all along?" I accused, sliding her bra straps down her arms before unhooking it and dropping it to the floor.

"To get you to suck the girls?" she asked. "Absolutely."

I grinned up at her as I rolled her nipples between my fingertips, pinching as I did. "You really think I should let them go?"

"Yeah, honey, I really think you should let them go," she said, leaning down to kiss me.

I dipped my hand under the waistband of her panties and slid it between her legs, slipping my fingers into her wet heat. Cricket dropped her head back and pressed her clit against my palm.

Just as a howl sounded through the baby monitor.

"No, no, no, no," Cricket whined as we both stalled.

"Be very still. Maybe he'll go back to sleep."

"Mama!" Cutter screamed.

She dropped her forehead to mine as I slid my hand out of her. "Shit."

"I'll get him," I said.

"No, I'll get him." She climbed off the bed and threw her shoes in the closet. "You fluff yourself and keep it hard."

I chuckled as she padded out of the room, just panties on, and I headed into the bathroom.

"Babe!" I heard through the monitor. "Little Cut's decided it's paint with poo time. I need backup."

I shook my head and made my way to Cutter's room, starting the bath on the way.

Fucking my wife into oblivion was going to have to wait.

* * *

Trouble

My phone buzzed at about eleven P.M., and when I saw it was Minus, I almost ignored it. Almost.

"Hey, Prez," I said.

"You can go."

"What?"

"You got my blessing," Minus said. "But I'm gonna tell you what I just told Taxi. I'm not bailing your ass out of any shit he gets you stuck in the middle of. The two of you are on your own. We'll discuss how and when you return to the club when he's done with his secret mission."

"Okay, thanks."

Minus hung up and I bit my lip.

Well, shit.

"Who was that?" Doozer asked.

God, I was so not ready to burst our love bubble. We'd had the best night in bed with ice cream and all the toppings that eventually ended up all over us instead of in our bowls. We'd just gotten out of the shower and I was hoping for another few hours of his magic dick.

"Minus. He wants me to look at a bike tomorrow," I lied.

"Right on," Doozer said, lifting me off my feet. "Time to get you dirty again."

"No more chocolate sauce in the puss," I begged. "That shit's hard to get out of the vag."

"I'll just have to do a better job of licking it all up."

I shivered, leaning down to kiss him. "Okay, honey, have at it."

He grinned and dropped me gently on the bed, his face moving between my legs, kissing one thigh, then the other.

He ran his tongue through my folds and hummed in surprise. "I don't taste chocolate anymore, baby. I think we got it all."

He reached for the chocolate syrup still on the nightstand, dripping a little on his fingertip and smearing in on my mound. He then licked it off and I gasped, arching into his touch.

"You wanna change your opinion about the chocolate?" Doozer teased.

I sat up slightly and held my hand out. "Give me the bottle."

"Why?"

"Because it's my turn." I slid off the mattress and knelt in front of Doozer. I wrapped my mouth around his dick and sucked gently.

He was already rock hard, so I squeezed a little syrup along his length and Doozer chuckled. "What the fuck are you doin'?"

"I'm making a banana split," I answered, spraying a little whipped cream over the top of the chocolate sauce.

"Jesus, that's cold."

I ran my tongue over his length, swallowing the sweetness as Doozer grew harder. "You taste good."

He ran his thumb over the apple of my cheek. "You rethinkin' the benefits of chocolate sauce?"

"Absolutely," I said, taking him in my mouth again, sucking as I slid my mouth back and forth, taking every ounce of the sweetness before finally giving him what he needed.

I drew him back into my mouth, taking his cock all the way to the back of my throat. I wrapped my hand around the base of his shaft and dragged it up and down as I kept working him with my mouth.

"Gonna fuck your mouth now," Doozer warned, and I nodded, squeezing him gently.

He gripped my scalp and began to rock. Slowly at first, then harder and harder, and I took him deeper and deeper. At one point, he was so deep, my eyes started to water.

I squeezed him gently, pulling back slightly, and Doozer slowed down. "You okay?" he grunted.

I nodded, pulling back enough to say, "Don't stop until you come."

He grinned. "Yes, ma'am."

I wrapped my lips back around him and he moved again, fucking my mouth until he gripped my scalp again as his body locked. He let out a quiet hiss, then I felt the warmth of his cum down my throat and I swallowed as his dick pulsated with this orgasm.

I released him with a quiet pop and grinned up at him. "I think you're tastier than stupid ol' chocolate."

He dropped his head back and laughed. "Jesus, you're perfect."

"Don't you ever forget it." I rose to my feet and Doozer wrapped his arms around me. I wove my fingers into his hair at the base of his neck.

"What did Minus really want?"

"Huh?"

"Don't 'huh' me," he ordered, gently. "I know when you lie to me, Stephanie. You have a tell."

"What?" I squeaked. "What kind of tell?"

"If I spill that information, you might be able to lie to me, so it's not happening." He cupped my face and kissed my nose. "So, tell me what Minus really said."

"He gave his permission for me to go to Virginia with Taxi."

"Fuck," Doozer breathed out.

"I thought you had my back."

"I do have your back," he said. "But that doesn't make you leaving me any easier."

"I'm not leaving you, Marco."

"What would you call it?"

"A business trip," I said. "For two months."

"A lot can happen in two months." He pulled away and stalked into the bathroom.

I bit my lip and leaned against the doorframe, watching him as he washed up. “It’ll go by faster than you think.”

“What about after?”

I sighed. “After training is done, you mean?”

Doozer nodded

“We’re gonna have to play those cards as they’re dealt to us. Are you okay with that?”

He dried his face and shook his head. “This is all gonna suck, baby, but I do have your back and we’ll figure it out. But please don’t expect me to be happy about it.”

I nodded. “I get it. It’s not like I’m looking forward to being apart from you, either.”

He closed the distance between us, leaning down to kiss me gently. “Let’s not talk about it anymore tonight. I just want to hold you and forget for a few hours.”

I stroked his cheek. “I love that idea.”

He smiled and took me back to bed.

Trouble

DOCTOR FENTON'S OFFICE, like most of what I'd seen of Quantico so far, was unremarkably plain. Bookcases and framed credentials lined the standard-issue beige walls. A few potted plants and some muted lighting attempted to soften the space, but if you've been in one government appointed therapist's office, you've been in them all.

"How was your flight?" Doctor Caroline Fenton

asked from her cozy looking chair.

"Fine," I replied softly. I was lying, of course. It was a seven-hour flight from Portland to Dulles, with a three-hour layover in Chicago, plus an additional one-hour drive to Quantico. We arrived at the academy at midnight, which meant it was three o'clock in the morning according to my body. I was wrecked. I'd barely slept, hadn't even had the chance to unpack my duffel bag, and here I was under the microscope of Quantico's chief psychologist at the ass crack of dawn.

"If you're jetlagged I have a wonderful tea I can make you," Doctor Fenton said, pointing to a small tea station in the corner.

"No, thank you. I'm fine," I said.

"You let me know if you change your mind," she said, sweetly. Doctor Caroline Fenton was beautiful and looked to be in her mid-thirties. "I can't seem to drink enough tea throughout the day." She pointed to what looked like a freshly poured cup on the small table beside her.

"Is the tea part of it?" I asked.

"Part of *what*?"

"Your test," I replied.

"I'm not sure I follow," Doctor Fenton said.

"The test to see if I'm psychologically fit to perform. Is whether or not I say yes to the tea a part of it?"

"No," she said, smiling. "There's no test. We're just here to talk."

"You mean, we're here to determine if I'm mentally stable enough to handle killing a person at the behest of the federal government."

Doctor Fenton patted the folder sitting on top of her desk. "Agent Davis's dossier on you says you're highly intelligent and speak directly. Seems accurate so far," she said with a smile.

"Oh, yeah? What else does it say?"

"That you are slow to trust people but are extremely loyal once you do. Is that true?"

I shrugged.

"Miss Palmer. I've known Agent Davis since he was a recruit and I've always known him to be an excellent judge of character. I agreed to meet with you personally at his request because I understand the time-sensitive nature of his training program. Even though you don't know me, I'd like to ask you to trust me."

"Trouble. Call me Trouble."

"Yes, of course," Doctor Fenton said warmly. "Whatever makes you comfortable."

"I'm not sure I've ever been more uncomfortable in my life," I said with a nervous laugh.

"Believe it or not, I too was once a fresh-faced recruit like you. There were even fewer female students in the academy back then and I was terrified my first day here. My first month, if I'm being honest. But soon enough, I felt like I'd been born and raised here."

"What changed?

"I lost an eye and the hearing in my right ear during a training accident," Doctor Fenton replied casually.

"What?"

"Yup," she said, removing her glasses and pulling her long blonde hair back to reveal a scar running from her ear to the corner of her eye. "This one's glass," she said pointing to her right eye.

"Holy shit," I blurted out. "I'm sorry, I—"

"That's okay," she said, shrugging. "If the accident had never happened, I'd be a field agent instead of a therapist, and I wouldn't trade what I do for the world."

"Can I ask what happened?" I asked.

"I took some friendly fire in Hogan's Alley," Doctor Fenton said, putting her glasses back on. She was stunning. Even with the scar, which was barely visible, especially behind her hair and glasses.

"Where's Hogan's Alley?"

Dr. Fenton smiled. "Hogan's Alley is one of our facilities here at Quantico. It's our very own small town within a small town. We use it for field training purposes. We can simulate everything from car chases to hostage situations. It was during one of those exercises that a fellow classmate discharged his weapon in close quarters. The slug ricocheted off the floor and struck me in the face."

"Oh, my God."

"I was lucky to be alive, but no longer fit for field duty after that, so I switched gears and studied to become a counselor for the bureau."

"And now you're the head of the entire department?"

"That's right."

"Do you ever wish you were a field agent?"

"I used to, in the beginning. But I love what I do more than anything and can't imagine doing anything else now."

"Wow," I said, now in complete awe of this beautiful blonde bombshell badass.

She leaned forward, seeming genuinely interested in what I had to say. "What about you? What's your superhero origin story?"

"I'm definitely not a superhero," I said.

"You certainly have a cool superhero name," she said. "How about we start with that? Did your club give you the name?"

I nodded. "Cowboy. The president of the first club I rode with, Bikers for Kids."

"Bikers for Kids?"

"It's a charity club that raises money and awareness

to prevent the cycle of child abuse and neglect," I replied.

"It sounds like you've said that a few times before," Dr. Fenton smiled.

"You learn to let those words come out quickly and easily when dealing with the public. People have a hard time trusting bikers, but if they know you work with kids, they relax a little bit."

"What type of work did you do with Bikers for Kids?"

"Toy drives, in-person visits, fundraising. Stuff like that."

"Did you find that type of work rewarding?"

"I did," I said, shifting in my seat.

"Are you uncomfortable talking about your work with Bikers for Kids?" Dr. Fenton asked, softly.

"More like uncomfortable talking about myself at all."

"I understand," she said.

"Plus, I never think about my time with BFK as work."

"It sounds like it must have been extremely hard work. Physically and emotionally. You strike me as a sensitive person, and I can't imagine you didn't take your experiences with those children home with you."

"I suppose Taxi mentions my father in that file."

Doctor Fenton nodded sympathetically. "I understand he passed away when you were quite young."

"No offense, Doc, but it's a little early in the day, and our doctor patient relationship to go there," I said.

"Fair enough," Doctor Fenton said.

"Maybe someday I could read the biography Taxi's written about me," I said, pointing the folder on her desk.

"I hope you don't feel like it's an invasion of your

privacy. I asked Agent Davis—"

"Taxi," I said. "Sorry to interrupt, but Taxi only wants us to use our club names when talking about each other. The first rule of undercover work."

"Of course," she said. "I asked *Taxi* to formulate his initial impressions of each team candidate so I could get up to speed as quickly as possible. Normally, we'd have an intake interview before training even began, and then I'd be able to get to know and evaluate you over the course of twenty weeks. But we don't have that kind of time."

"I get it." I sighed. "It's just kinda creepy, that's all."

"I'll be happy to make a copy for you after our session."

"Really? That's not classified information or anything?"

"I think we'll be okay," she said with a wink. "Can we return to the topic of your time with Bikers for Kids?"

"Not much to tell," I replied. "What do you want to know?"

"From what I've read, and what you've said this morning, I get the impression you enjoyed riding with them. Why did you quit them and join the Burning Saints?"

"It's not quite like that. I didn't quit BFK. I was a patch over."

"What's a patch over?"

"Sometimes, a trusted member of an MC is allowed to transition from their club into another club. Sometimes entire clubs do it."

"Is that sort of thing done a lot within the biker community?"

"The *biker community*? You make us sound like a voter demographic," I said with a chuckle.

"I'm sorry. I didn't mean to offend you."

My chuckle turned to a laugh. "I think you'd have to stab me with that letter opener to offend me."

"Let's hope our conversations stay puncture wound free," Dr. Fenton said, steering the conversation back on course. "You were explaining being a patch over."

"Yeah, it's not super common, I guess, but both Cowboy and Minus thought it was a good idea, so I was cool with it."

An eyebrow raised over the rim of Doctor Fenton's glasses. "Simple as that?"

"What do you mean?"

"You don't strike me as the kind of person who'd simply let two men trade you like a baseball card."

"It was nothing like that," I protested.

"Then if it was your decision, I'd love to know why you made it?"

"Why is it important for you to know that?"

"I'm more than happy to answer that question, Trouble, but I'm afraid I would need to bring up a topic you've requested to address on another day."

"My dad?"

Dr. Fenton nodded.

"What does my dad have to do with who I ride with?"

"I suspect he has a great deal to do with many of the choices you've made, not the least of which being here at Quantico, training as a sniper."

"The training as a sniper bit isn't lost on me," I admitted.

She smiled slightly.

"Riding with BFK probably has something to do with the fact I never want a child to ever feel like a burden, especially during the holidays when it's painfully evident they have nothing." I picked at a nonexistent piece of lint on my jeans. "Patching over to the Saints is more complicated."

"Oh?" Dr. Fenton hummed. "How so?"

I squirmed in my chair for a few tense seconds before blurting out, "I fell in love."

* * *

Doozer

Life without Trouble was literally becoming painful. Every morning I'd wake with a swollen cock, hard enough to pound railroad spikes. Of course, I wanted to be pounding Trouble, but with her gone, my only current options were my hand, and one of the strippers from last night's party that were no doubt passed out in various places within the Sanctuary.

Kitty's birthday bash was last night, and although Minus had tried to steer the club away from strippers, Warthog elegantly pointed out, "It ain't no Kitty party if it ain't no titty party," so we acquiesced. Of course, stripper parties usually ended in orgies and last night was no exception. Silicone and glitter not quite being my thing, I escaped to my room with a bottle, wishing I could call Trouble.

I drank myself into oblivion instead, and after hauling my ass out of bed this morning, I nearly rammed my dick into the side of the shower as I stepped under the water. I was gonna have to take care of this myself.

Taking my cock into my hand, I slid my palm up my aching shaft, dropping my head back with a groan. I thought of Trouble's perfect lips wrapped around my throbbing dick, the hot water serving as a substitute for her tongue. I stroked myself faster as I imagined her taking me deeper and deeper into her mouth. My thigh muscles tightening as I quickened the pace. My mind flooding with memories of times Trouble had happily sucked me off. Kneeling, with her eyes locked on mine as my cock filled her greedy mouth. As Trouble's fantasy blow job continued, I pumped my cock harder, bringing me closer and closer to the edge until I finally exploded. Imagining Trouble taking every drop into her mouth as I came.

Finally, I could start the day with a little relief.

Trouble

BY WEEK FOUR, life at Quantico had settled into the kind of rhythm a blacksmith falls into when hammering a sword into shape. In this scenario, I was most certainly the hunk of iron. Repeatedly heated up and hammered. Bashed into shape until I began to resemble something even I didn't recognize.

Every day, after morning chow, I'd meet with Dr. Fenton for one hour. We'd talk, I'd cry, then I'd get pissed off at her for making me cry. She'd tell me that it wasn't really her that I was angry with and yada, yada,

yada. Dr. Fenton always looked pleased at the end of our sessions, and would say encouraging things like, "Thank you for your honesty," and "You're doing great," but the sessions with her were like going through an emotional meat grinder.

However, much to my surprise, I found myself looking forward to our talks. I'm not sure if it was due to her training, or something about her specifically, but Dr. Fenton had the ability to crack me open like a walnut, while still making me feel safe.

After the morning's emotional pounding, I'd join the team for course work, which was usually led by a guest instructor. One day, we'd learn from an explosives expert about identifying types of bombs and I.E.D.s in the field. The next day, it would be a medic teaching us how to do C.P.R. Every morning it was something new, and another section of both my brain, and notebook filled up. After that, the team would have lunch together in the mess, then head off to the field training location of the day.

This was always the most exciting and nerve-wracking part of the day. Three days ago, I found myself harnessed into a rig that simulated being submerged in water while trapped inside a vehicle. The rig and I were plunged into a pitch-black swimming pool filled with nearly freezing cold water and I had only a multi-tool to free myself. Despite being terrified, I managed to complete the exercise within the allotted time, and without drowning.

Today we were running drills in Hogan's Alley and I was in the hot seat. More specifically the "God Seat," a term used by snipers to describe the shooter with the highest vantage point. I was positioned on top of a building made to look like a New York brownstone. My teammates, Tackle and Boots, were down the block, waiting outside a mock coffee shop. Taxi, along with the rest of our team, were observing silently from an unknown location.

Tackle, Boots, and I were running a training scenario in which we, the blue team, were acting as undercover agents making a large drug buy from a new supplier. The drug traffickers were played by seasoned Quantico instructors who held every possible advantage over us. The red team were seasoned veterans who knew every inch of Hogan's Alley like the back of their hands, and they took no mercy on us. These exercises were child's play to them, and so far, they'd handed our asses to us every time we went up against them. I was determined not to lose to them again.

My orders were to spot and identify any incoming forces and take them out should they engage first. I felt confident about the spot I'd chosen and a clear scope all the way down to my team. If these drug-running assholes tried anything, I was ready to light them up.

"Blue leader. A black SUV is heading your way, approaching from the west," I said into the mic sewn into my collar. Our clothing was wired for sound enabling us to communicate with one another via wireless mics and earpieces.

"Copy that, Jehovah," Tackle replied. "Confirmed, a bogie is headed our way."

Tackle was the senior member of our team in all regards. He was the oldest, the first to be recruited by Taxi, and the one we looked to as our leader, whether he liked it or not. He rode with the Killing Jokers out of Florida, who were as old school as they came. He never talked about how he came to be on Taxi's team, but I got the feeling it was for reasons more personal than business.

"Shit, man. An SUV? There's no telling how many

guys could be in there," Boots said with a groan.

"Yup," Tackle replied.

"Don't worry, boys. God sees you and loves you very much," I said, keeping my rifle trained on my team.

The SUV pulled up to the spot where Tackle and Boots were waiting, and four bad guys got out. One of them was carrying a metal briefcase.

"I have eyes on the package," Tackle said.

"You're right on time," the red leader said, casually approaching my team.

"And you're late," Tackle said.

"What can I say, traffic this time of day is a bitch," he said, motioning to the empty streets of Hogan's Alley.

"What's with all the guys?" Tackle asked.

The exercises Taxi had us running were designed to help us hone our undercover skills as much as our technical skills. We were to stay in character at all times during training, as if our lives depended upon it.

"Don't worry about them," the red leader said, motioning to the three men behind him. "They're here for my peace of mind."

"You named the time and place and we're here. No bullshit, just like I said. So, we gonna do this or what?" Tackle asked.

"You got the money?" the red leader asked.

"It's in the trunk," Tackle said, pointing to the beat-up nineties Honda Accord training vehicle parked in front of the "coffee shop."

Hogan's Alley looked less like a training facility and more like the back lot of Hollywood movie studio, and if you didn't look too closely at the buildings' façades you'd swear you were in an actual town.

"How about you have your buddy there get it out of

the trunk, nice and slow and we'll make the exchange right here?" the red leader said.

"You heard him," Tackle said to Boots. "Get the bag out of the car."

"Nice and slow. So, I can see you," the red leader said.

"We heard you. Take it easy," Tackle said. "I told you, we're straight. No tricks."

"Yeah, well I don't know you and I don't like to take chances."

Just then, I spotted a second black SUV round the corner of the drop location, parking just out of view of my scope. My heart raced at the complication and I had to think fast.

"Damnit," I hissed, switching my mic on. "Blue leader, you're gonna have company. An identical SUV just pulled up to the east corner. I have lost visual on it. Repeat, I have lost visual."

I knew Tackle wouldn't be able to respond without blowing his cover but hoped he could at least hear me.

"Hold up," Tackle said to the red team leader. "I'm a cautious man myself, so how 'bout you let me see the product before we go any further."

"That's not how this works. You bring me the money, and we give you the product," the red leader said, his tone becoming more aggressive.

"Jerry said this would be a no hassle deal," Tackle said. "What the fuck is this?"

"I sure hope you're not thinking of backing out, because that wouldn't be very smart of you."

"Yeah? Well, I'm thinkin' that might be the smartest thing I do all day. Come on, Boots," Tackle said, motioning for his partner to get in the car.

"I said backing out wasn't a good idea," the red leader said, pulling out a pistol, leveling it at my team.

I clicked off the rifle's safety.

"Be cool, and we can all just walk away, here," Tackle said, calmly.

"Don't worry. I'll be walking away as soon as you give me that bag full of money."

"I told you. Deal's off," Tackle said.

"This isn't a deal anymore, now gimmie the bag."

"You really think we're here alone?" Tackle asked. "You pull that trigger and you're a dead man."

"You brought guys with guns. I brought guys with guns." The red leader motioned to his goons. "We could turn the place into a bloodbath, sure. But you're not gonna," he said, just as the second SUV rounded the corner, the door swinging open to reveal Jette, bound and gagged in the back seat.

"Make one move and the driver shoots her, *Agent* Tackle," the red leader said.

Taxi had obviously handed Jette over to the red team to be used as a hostage. He loved to throw curveballs during these exercises. Still, I had to play this scenario out as if it were real. After some quick figuring and a quick prayer to whoever might be listening, I slowed my breathing, put the target in my crosshairs, and let my mind go blank.

In that moment, and possibly for the first time in my life, I trusted myself. In that split second, I decided on a plan, executed it, and felt confident that I'd made the right call. I didn't act out of fear, impulse, or even the desire to beat the red team. Only to do what was best for my team.

I held my breath and squeezed the trigger, activating the sensor in the driver's hat, indicating a head shot. I targeted red leader and fired a second shot, hitting him center mass, giving Tackle and Boots time to draw their weapons on the three remaining bad guys and take them into custody.

I was told most of this afterward, as I'd missed most of the event myself. I saw only flurries of activity in my scope as my mind swam in and out of a fugue state. I was aware I'd decided to take the shots, but after that, it was like I was on auto pilot.

After a moment of silence, I heard the celebratory whoops and hollers of my fellow teammates in my earpiece, followed by Taxi's voice. "Blue team, report to rendezvous point Charlie immediately."

My team was there to greet me by the time I'd packed my rifle and returned to the street level. I almost felt like I'd left another version of myself on that rooftop. Pride wasn't a feeling I was accustomed to, but the looks on Tackle, Boots, and Jette's faces made my heart swell.

"Holy shit! I've never seen anything like that in my entire fuckin' life. I swear to god!" Tackle shouted excitedly.

"Seriously," Boots said. "How the hell do you manage to get off two clean shots from that distance?"

"Because she's a badass," the usually reserved Jette screamed, giving me a huge hug.

"Thank you, guys," I said, knowing I was fully blushing and not caring at all. For once, I couldn't wait for our debrief with Taxi. I kept my shit together, did my job, and helped lead my team to victory.

"Congratulations on another failed mission, blue team," Taxi said, throwing the field report to the ground.

"What the fuck?" I blurted out.

"Did you say something, candidate?" Taxi bellowed.

The entire team stood in line, at attention, while Taxi paced back and forth in front of us like a drill sergeant.

"No, sir," I replied, wanting to crawl inside myself.

"I didn't fucking think so," he snapped. I'd never seen Taxi this angry. which only added to my confusion. I thought Taxi would be all hugs and high fives, but instead I'm worried about getting kicked out of the program.

"Now, would one of you like to tell me what the hell happened out there today?"

"Trouble took out two bad guys and saved all our asses," Tackle said.

"Is that right? Is that what happened?" Taxi asked, turning his attention to Boots. "Is that how you see it?"

"Actually, yeah," Boots said.

"Well, please allow me to inform all of you exactly all of the ways you're *dead fucking wrong*," he shouted, before turning to me. "Trouble, what was blue team's mission?"

"To make contact with the red team and exchange money for drugs," I replied.

"For what purpose?"

My palms were sweating, and I felt like I was gonna pass out. "F…for the p…purpose of furthering the relationship between ours…selves and the sellers."

"Very good. That's right," Taxi said, cheerily. "Now, let me ask a follow up question. How fucking good do you think our relationship is with them now that their brains are splattered all over *fucking Main Street*?"

"The deal had gone south," I protested.

"Are you completely sure about that? In the training scenario, these were first-time buyers, right?"

I nodded.

"In the real world, sellers test buyers they don't know very well. Who's to say the display of power on the part of the red team wasn't all just part of a test?"

"They were holding Jette hostage," I pointed out.

"That's how you saw it from two-hundred meters away."

"Boss, that's how it looked on the ground too," Tackle said.

Taxi stopped pacing and turned to face us all. "You know, for a bunch of criminals, you sure think like cops. You must start thinking outside the box. Jette may have been a hostage, and she may have been a double agent, working with the cartel. Perhaps, she was loyal to blue team and was working on a strategy of her own. There were still many options on the table that could have led to a successful outcome, but Trouble's itchy trigger finger eliminated all of them."

"I was protecting my team," I said, trying to hide the quiver in my voice.

"You made the wrong call," Taxi said, unsympathetically. "In the real world, your little Annie Oakley routine would have torched an ongoing operation, exposed your team, and left two dead bodies in the street. If that's not a failure I don't know what it is."

Doozer

IT HAD BEEN a month since Trouble left and I was climbing the walls. There was no place on Sanctuary grounds that didn't feel haunted. No matter where I went, something reminded me of her, and it was driving me crazy. I needed to get the hell out of here and find something else to occupy my mind for a while.

My phone buzzed and I picked it up to see a text from my sister, Gia. I was about to get a bigger distraction than I ever could have imagined.

Gia: The family is having an impromptu lunch at Vincenzo's today at 1:00. It won't be the same without you. Please say you'll join us.

I started to type that I wouldn't be able to make it but stopped. As much as I dreaded the thought of lunch with my father, I did miss my sisters and mother. I'd successfully managed to dodge every family get together since Trouble and I hooked up but knew that couldn't last forever. Eventually I'd have to see my family again, and once they knew about Trouble, they'd want an introduction, but the mere thought of subjecting Trouble to my family made my feet sweat. At least with Trouble currently out of town, I could check in with my family without opening that can of worms.

Two hours later I was shown to my family's usual table at Vincenzo's Fine Italian Eatery where my father was waiting for me, alone.

"What the fuck do you mean Mama and the girls aren't joining us?"

"Please, Marco. Do you have to use that kind of language? Especially here, at Vincenzo's. It's our family restaurant."

"Yeah, Pop. *Family*. Which is who I agreed to have lunch with. So where are the rest of them?"

"Sit down. Sit down," My father said. "You always make such a scene. You're like your mother."

"I'll take that as a compliment," I said, reluctantly taking the seat at the far end of the table, just as two bussers came to the table and removed the place servings set out for the mother and sisters. "They were never coming, were they?" I asked.

"Marco, it's time for you and me to sit down and have a chat, don't you think?"

"Clearly you do," I said, dryly.

"Please, son. This is important to me," he said.

"If it's so damned important to you, why not just call and ask me to meet with you instead of having Gia set up some phony family lunch?"

"Would you have said yes if I'd invited you? Would you have even answered the phone?"

I gave my father a slight shrug.

"Don't be angry with your sister, she only did what I asked her to do."

"I'm not pissed at Gia. I'm pissed at you."

"Please, Marco. Hear me out. We've been at war for far too long, but I have something that I hope will bring peace between us."

"Where'd you find enough paper to write out an apology list that long?"

"Again, Marco. Even if I did write an apology to you, would you read it?"

"What the fuck is that supposed to mean?" I snapped.

"Son, please. Your language."

"This is why we don't talk. Because you try to control everything I say and do. I curse, Pop. Get over it. I have tattoos. I ride a bike and belong to an MC. This is who I am."

"What if it wasn't, son? What if I could offer you more?"

"More what?" I asked.

"Everything," my father said, with a passion he usually reserved for when he was in court. "More of everything life has to offer."

"Pop, I thought I was coming here to have lunch with the family. I don't have time for bullshit games," I said, standing to leave.

"Marco, I want to offer you a job. It's a position that is especially important to me, and one that you will come to see is in your best interest to take."

"What the hell are you taking about? What position? You're retired now."

"Sit down, have lunch with me, and I'll fill you in on all the details. Once you hear what I have to say, you can decide whether to stay or go."

"I can decide that right now," I snapped.

"Marco, please," my father said softly. His arms outstretched to the table.

Maybe it was the rare expression of vulnerability on his face, but against my better judgement I did as my father asked. Throwing my weight down on the chair like a pissed off teenager.

"Thank you," my father sighed. "Shall we order first?" He asked, waiving a waiter to our table before waiting for my response.

"Good afternoon, Mr. Mancini. It's always nice to have you with us," the waiter said, handing us menus.

"I'll have the Veal Parmigiana and an Arnold Palmer please, Jake," my father said.

"Very good, and for you, sir," Jake asked, turning to me.

"I'll have a beer," I said. "Something imported and large."

"Certainly, sir," Jake said, making a hasty retreat to the kitchen.

I could tell my father was itching to make a comment, but instead took a beat before restarting.

"Now, as I was saying. Now that I'm retired from practicing law, I have time to focus on my other business interests."

"I didn't know you had other business interests."

"I started investing in commercial real estate right around the time Carmen was born," he said, and my mind went to the documents Kitty had discovered in his investigation of Judge Snodgrass. Whatever this was about must have something to do with their dealings together.

"Real estate, huh?" I asked.

"Yes, but always as a silent partner. I never had time for more. The firm and the family kept me more than busy."

"*The firm* kept you busy," I corrected.

"You're probably right, son. I'm sure there were times when I did work too many hours. And maybe I didn't spend as much time with you as I should have. But now I can change all that."

My father's attempt at an apology, or whatever this was, made me feel far more uncomfortable than when he'd lay into me.

"What is this all about?" I asked.

"I told you. I want to offer you a job."

"I already have a job. I build bikes."

"Marco, my goal is to extend an olive branch. To offer you a position that could expand your world far beyond that of a mechanic's."

"I'm not a mechanic. I'm a custom bike builder." I snapped. "The work I do requires artistry and precision. I happen to be extremely proud of what I do, even if you aren't. I'm also paid well for the work I do."

"Do you earn enough to start a family and buy a house in Portland?"

"Who says that's what I want? And who says it's any of your damned business either way?"

"I'm your father," he said in a matter-of-fact tone.

"And you don't know anything about me," I challenged.

"That's not true. I may not know everything about you, but if you think I haven't kept tabs on what my only son has been up to over the years, you don't yet know the depth of a father's love."

"*A father's love?* Are you fucking kidding me? When did you ever show me an ounce of your love?

You spent my entire life either ignoring or disapproving of me."

"You're wrong, son. I've spent my life working in order to provide for you and your sisters. That's how I showed my love. And I may disapprove of your lifestyle, but not of you. Not of the man I know you can still become."

"My *lifestyle*, as you call it, *is* who I am. That's what you don't get, Pop."

My father's tone shifted from personal to business. "I'm offering you a starting salary of two-hundred and fifty-thousand dollars a year."

"What?" I exclaimed, a little louder than I'd planned.

"Plus, six weeks paid leave and an annual performance bonus."

"To do what?"

"Logistics management."

At this point I began to worry that my father was suffering from dementia.

"I don't even know what a logistic is let alone how you manage one," I said. "I don't even know what this business of yours is."

"I'm in the middle of negotiating a land deal that is bigger and far more lucrative than anything I've been part of before."

Of course, I was aware my father had some sort of land deal cooking with Judge Snodgrass, but I wasn't about to let him know about my intel.

"Congratulations, but I still don't see what any of that has to do with me," I said.

"This deal involves you, because once it's completed, your future children, my grandchildren, will be set up for life," my father said, excitedly. "And I want all of my children to work with me to help make it happen. As soon as we enter the next phase of development, I'll be bringing Gia and Carmen on as the company's private legal team, but I need you to make that happen."

"Gia and Carm can do what they want, but I've never asked for your money and I don't need it."

"It's not about the money, Marco. It's about our family building something together. A legacy."

"I still don't understand how I could possibly help you," I said.

"I'm bound by an iron-clad non-disclosure agreement, unable to say much more until you're on the payroll, but let me assure you, son. You are in a unique position to help your family become a dynasty in Portland."

"Through logistics fucking management?"

"You have to trust me when I say you have all the education and experience needed to fill this position and that it is in your best interest to accept it."

"That almost sounded like a threat," I said.

"Not at all," my father replied. "Believe it or not, Marco, I care deeply about your future."

I studied my father's face. He seemed genuine but was clearly withholding as much as he was disclosing. However, his reluctance to give me detailed information about this deal was far less shocking than the fact that he wanted me involved in the first place.

"Take some time over the next few days to think about my offer," my father said. "Maybe talk things over with that girl of yours."

"What?"

My father grinned. "I told you, son. I hear things."

* * *

"The order sheet says high gloss finish," Elwood repeated.

"I already told you I don't give a shit what the order

sheet says. I talked to Jeff yesterday, and he definitely wants a satin finish."

"But he signed the sheet, and the sheet says glossy." Elwood held up his clipboard.

"I swear to God, Wood. If you show me that thing one more time, I'm gonna shove it so far up your ass—"

"I'd like to see you try, punk," he said tossing his clipboard onto the nearby workbench and getting into a fighting stance.

"Don't get yourself all worked up, old man," I retorted. "I'd hate for you to break a hip doing all that Kung-Fu fighting."

"My bones are fuckin' fine, and so are my eyes. The order says glossy. It's candy apple red for fuck's sake."

"I'm fully aware of the client's color and finish choice. I'm also aware the order sheet is incorrect. If you want to call Jeff and look like a disorganized, unprofessional jackass, be my fuckin' guest. Here I'll dial his number for you," I said, picking up the shop phone, just as Minus walked in.

"Hey, it's my favorite show," he said excitedly. "The Real Housewives of Portland. What are you two bitches fighting about now?"

"Nothing a phone call can't solve," I said, waiving the receiver in front of Elwood.

"Fine," he said, taking the receiver from me and slamming down. "But who the hell ever heard of candy apple red in satin?"

"Welcome to the twenty-first century, Wood."

"I barely fuckin' liked the twentieth," he grumbled, before returning to the paint booth, slamming the door behind him.

"Nice to see Elwood in a good mood for a change," Minus said, before handing me a plain white envelope. "This came for you."

I opened it to find a letter from Trouble.

"Everything okay?" Minus asked.

"I'm not sure. I'm gonna take a break and read this while Elwood gets the booth set up," I said, holding up the letter.

"Sure thing," Minus replied.

I exited the shop and headed for the grove of trees by the old pump house. I sat down under the hundred-year-old pines on a stone bench built by who knows who, back in who knows when. This was my favorite spot on the Saints' property. Something about the age of the trees and the anonymity of the stoneworker who built the bench was humbling. It made me and my problems feel insignificant in a comforting way. I unfolded the pages and read, unsure if I'd find a love note or Dear John letter.

In the end, it was neither and it was both.

Doozer
I've sat down to write this letter three times (okay, maybe four). It started as an exercise given to us by Taxi. Well, more of a command, really, and I figured I could just send you a note telling you everything's cool, I miss you, and move on with my day.
I can't.

I miss you. I miss you like crazy, baby, and this is where the problem and heartache lay, because I cannot have that distraction. I'm deep in the shit now, and it's exactly where I'm supposed to be. But in the middle of that deep shit, you'll take a leisurely stroll through my mind and I'm distracted. Maybe for a second, maybe for a minute, but it's long enough to scare me. If I'm out 'there' and distracted, lives get lost, and I could never forgive myself. Right now, I just want to crawl into your arms and stay there forever, but that's probably because I've had two hours of sleep and I'm a little emotional after my session with Dr. Fenton.

I had no fucking clue who Dr. Fenton was, but I already hated his fucking guts. I forced myself to finish the letter even if my heart was shattering.

Jesus, I'm rambling, even in a letter. Sorry. I don't really know what I'm trying to say, I just know that this isn't something that can continue. Not the way it's been going, anyway. I wish I could see or hear you, but maybe this is exactly the way it's supposed to be. I don't know. I don't really have any answers. Please stay safe and know that I will always love you. ~ Trouble.

Doozer

I HURRIED BACK to the shop and was surprised to find Minus still there, waiting for me.

"Everything okay?" I asked.

"I was gonna ask you the same thing," he said, pointing to Trouble's letter, still in my hand.

"Uh. Yeah. Everything's good," I said, opening my locker and tossing the letter inside. I reached for my painting suit, only to find it missing from its hook. "You stupid fucking idiot," I growled at myself. Slamming my fist into the locker next to mine, I dented the shit out of it.

"Whoa," Minus said, walking over to me. "You don't sound okay."

"I forgot my painting suit. I left it soaking in the sink, even though I reminded myself to take it out a hundred fucking times."

"Then Spike's locker definitely had it coming," he said, dryly.

"Sorry, man," I said, putting my hands in the air. "I'll fix it."

"It's no big deal," Minus said. "I'm more worried about where your head is at."

"A million fuckin' miles away, lately," I said.

"More like twenty-eight-hundred," Minus said with a smile, pointing again at Trouble's letter, now at the bottom of my locker. "And if that letter says what your face says it says, I suspect I have to decide."

"Decide what?" I asked.

"Whether or not to let you go to Quantico," he replied.

"Why would you let me do that?"

"First of all because it would piss off Taxi," Minus said with a chuckle. "Secondly, because I need to send someone out to Savanah anyway, and you could stop off in Virginia for a few days on your way out. Mostly, because when I was your age, Cutter never gave me the chance to work things out between Cricket and me. And although I'm happy with how things turned out for us in the end, I still wish I had those lost years back. And, like I said." Minus smiled wide. "It'll piss Taxi off."

"I feel like Trouble doesn't need me," I said.

"Trouble may not need you. Hell, she may not need anyone. But she sure as shit loves you. That's easy to see. And I don't know what she's going through in the least bit, but I'd bet the club, she'd be able to face it better if you were there to remind her how strong she is."

"Thanks, Prez. I don't know what to say."

"This isn't a vacation. Just a layover on a business trip. Got it?"

"Loud and clear," I replied.

"Good, 'cause there's one more thing you need to take care of before you go and you aren't gonna like it."

"What's goin' on?"

"Kitty's just brought me up to speed with this land deal your father's involved with."

"Yeah, I already talked to him about it. He offered me a job. It's nothing. Just family drama bullshit. I told him to fuck off."

"Yeah, well it seems *your* family drama has now become *our* family drama."

"How so?"

"Do you know who your father's doing business with?"

I frowned. "All I know is he got Judge Snodgrass to greenlight a project with some company called Mayflower something or other—"

"A land development deal," Minus said.

"Yeah," I confirmed.

"Do you happen to know where that land is located?"

"Dad never mentioned it, so why would I care where the land is located?" I bit out.

"You'd care if you knew that Judge Snodgrass is attempting to claim imminent domain on the land the Burning Saints currently call the Sanctuary."

"What the fuck?"

"And that's not all, junior. If what Kitty's shown me is correct, the Mayflower Development Corporation is backed entirely by the Beast."

"How often is Kitty wrong?" I asked, my heart dropping.

“Never. Which is why I need you to squash this shit.”

“How am I supposed to do that?” I asked.

“He’s your father,” Minus said. “You need to give it to him straight for his own protection as well as the club’s. I don’t know why he’s in bed with the Beast, or how much he knows about them, but if you can’t convince him to pull the plug on this deal, I’m gonna have to get involved.”

Minus didn’t have to say anything more.

“I’ll take care of this tonight,” I said.

“Good. Now go borrow someone else’s suit and help Elwood in the painting booth before he fucks up another order.”

I gave Minus a nod and did as I was told.

Doozer

I SAT OUTSIDE my parents' house and revved my bike's engine as loud as I could. My father came rushing out of the house scowling, followed by mother. Her hands covering her ears.

I killed the motor and removed my helmet.

"Marco, what is this? Why all the noise?" my mother asked. "I thought it was the end of the world."

"I'm sorry, Ma. I didn't mean to upset you. I just need to talk to Pop, that's all."

"Normal people call," my father said. "They don't disturb the neighbors with a lot of racket."

"Sorry, Pop, did you say racket or rackets?" I asked, my eyes locked on my father. "I know you've got some new friends who are into some… interesting stuff."

"Go on inside, Marisa," my father said, kissing my mother's forehead. "Marco and I are gonna talk out here for a minute. I'll be back inside before my coffee gets cold."

"Okay," my mother said. "But no more noise with that motorbike," she said, scurrying back to the house.

"What the hell is all this about, Marco?"

"You know it's not a good idea to drink coffee at night. It can fuck with your sleep," I said, climbing off my bike.

"Is that why you're here? To give me advice on how to sleep better?"

"Actually, I'm curious how the fuck you manage to sleep at all," I said, pulling Kitty's file from my saddle bag. "Doing business with criminals, and all."

"What on earth are you talking about?" My father asked, scanning the pages in the file. "What is this? How did you get these documents?"

"How I got them isn't nearly as important as what's in them," I said.

"These documents are my business," my father bellowed, before quickly lowering his voice.

"No, Pop. It's okay. I want your neighbors to hear this. After all, it's their approval you've been seeking all along, isn't it? They should know who you really are."

"What are you talking about, Marco?"

"You've spent so much time building up your precious reputation as some sort of pillar of the community. Caring only about what complete strangers think about you. Ashamed of your own son because he didn't conform to your version of what it means to be a man. Living behind a phony code of ethics. But it's all a lie,

Pop."

"Marco, you don't understand how the business world works—"

"No, Pop. It's you who doesn't understand. These people you're doing business with are criminals."

"No, no, see," my father said smiling. Pointing to one of the documents. "You're wrong, I'm working with Reggie Snodgrass on this. You know, the appellate court judge."

"Yeah, I know. Through his daughter's development company."

"That's right, his daughter Patricia," my father confirmed.

"Since when are you so chummy with the Snodgrass family?"

"Reggie approached me right around the time I announced my retirement. He said he had a deal that would secure my retirement and asked if I'd be interested in investing."

"And you didn't find it odd that a judge you've had nothing but contempt for in the past just happened to have a deal he wanted to cut you in on?"

"Like I said, Marco. The business world is often complicated."

"How complicated was it to set up that off-shore account? Or did the judge do that for you?"

"Is that what this is about? The tax shelter Patricia helped me set up?"

"Tax shelter? Are you fucking kidding me, Pop? Or should I say Leo Vox?"

"Please, son. Keep your voice down," my father begged.

"We could talk inside if you'd rather," I said, pointing to the house. "I'd love to find out how much Mama knows about all of this."

"I don't want you upsetting your mother any more tonight."

"Tell me, Pop. How much is it going to upset Mama when you go to jail for real estate fraud and tax evasion?"

"I don't know where you're getting all these crazy ideas."

"Pop," I said, placing my hands on my father's shoulders. "The people you're dealing with are as dirty as they come. The judge and his daughter are working with a criminal organization called the Beast, who are basically the new breed of the Dixie Mafia. The Beast is bankrolling the judge's portion of the land buy, in exchange for his political influence within the Mayor's office and the city council."

"I don't know where you heard such a crazy story, but I can assure you, I'm merely an investor—"

"In a real estate investment deal for the sale of the land my club currently occupies," I said.

"What are you talking about? The land we're acquiring is all undeveloped commercial space. We're working with the city to rezone the area as residential, then we can begin construction on our condos."

"You'll have to forgive me if the thought of building condos on top of the Sanctuary doesn't excite me."

"Son, I can assure you. I have no idea what you're talking about."

"No way," I said. "You're way too smart not to have seen what was going on. This is all part of a plan to get the Burning Saints out of Portland…" I paused, my blood turning to ice water. "The job," I said.

"What?"

"The job you offered me. What did you call it? Logistics Manager?"

My father nodded.

"You wanted me to help you."

"Son, you have to understand. I—"

"You son of a bitch. You wanted to hire me to help you kick my club off their land."

"Land purchased with blood money," he snapped.

"Holy shit. I was right," I said. "Judge Snodgrass is going to claim imminent domain so the city can acquire the land for pennies on the dollar. The city will then sell the land to Mayflower who will in turn build condos, car parks, and a shopping center.

"The Burning Saints are criminals who've taken from the city of Portland for too long," my father sneered.

"The Burning Saints are my family."

"*We* are your family! *I* am your family, Marco, and that motorcycle gang took you from me!" he shouted. "They took you from me and turned your heart against me."

"I can't believe you thought I'd go along with you. That I would put a bullet in the back of my own club."

"Your club's days are numbered in Portland. If it's not this mayor who drives you out, it'll be the next one. At least this way, your club stands to make enough money to set up shop someplace else."

"And, what? I stay here and work with dear old dad, punching a clock at the Mayflower Development Group?"

"I told you, son. You'd be set up financially. You wouldn't have to work for that gang anymore. This will be good for all of us. Don't you see?"

"The only thing I see is a delusional old man who's in way over his head," I said. "You need to understand that Snodgrass is not your friend or even your business associate. He's a corrupt judge who's under the thumb of the new breed of the Dixie Mafia. He's only using you to get to our club."

"Why would he do that?"

"Because the Beast wants to set up shop in Portland and believe me that's the last thing you want. You're right, the Burning Saints don't have the cleanest record and we've spilled our share of blood, but that's not who we're trying to be anymore. And believe me when I tell you, that apart from some friends in high places, the Saints are the only ones keeping the Beast from running roughshod over Portland right now."

"Even if you're right, there's nothing I can do about it now. The deal's already in motion."

"Then you'd better find a way to grind it to a halt within the next forty-eight hours or I'll turn you into the police myself."

My father stared at me in disbelief.

"I told you, Pop. My business is legit, and I have nothing to hide. Can you say the same?"

"I just wanted us to be a family again," he said softly.

"Kill the deal, Pop," I said. "'Cause if you don't, I will, and I'll make sure you go down with the Snodgrasses, the Beast, and everyone else who thought it was a good idea to fuck with my club."

* * *

By the time I rode back to the Sanctuary, my eyeballs ached, and my head was pounding. Of all the shitty things I could imagine my father doing, I never could have imagined him becoming a criminal and joining forces with my enemy in order to destroy my club.

Angry and exhausted I made it to my room, slumped onto my bed in a heap, pulled out my phone, and called Minus.

"How'd it go?" he asked, picking up immediately.

"Okay, I guess."

"Were you able to find out anything more?"

"I'm not sure how much he knows," I said. "It appears I may know a lot more than he did. He actually seemed surprised by some of the shit I told him."

"You could have blind spots, though. Him being your old man and all."

"Trust me. I'm the last person who's gonna come to my father's defense. He knows enough to be guilty in my eyes, but I think the Beast and Judge Snodgrass played him."

"Where does that leave us?"

"I told my father he had forty-eight hours to kill the deal with the judge. Without Pop's cooperation and the use of his offshore account, the deal can't proceed."

"Do you think he'll listen to you?"

"I told him he either parts ways with judge Snodgrass or with his freedom. The choice is his."

"Could you really turn him in to the cops?"

"My father's too proud to face a scandal. He'll do what's right and kill the deal."

"The Beast will figure out another way to come at us, but at least this buys us some time. Good job, Doozer. I'll see you when you get back from your trip."

Trouble

I WANTED TO take it back. All of it. I wanted to retract my letter and start again, hit the backspace on the computer of my life, but I couldn't. It was gone, and now that I'd had a full night's sleep, I had a feeling Doozer was going to lose his shit, assume I'd dumped him, and fuck some club whore to feel better. If I could just get access to a phone, maybe I could explain.

But that was a no-go. Taxi had taken our phones when we'd gotten here, and the only calls we could make were pre-approved and monitored. A couple of the recruits had attempted to sneak in burners, but Taxi seemed to know all the tricks and they were confiscated quickly, so a call with Doozer wasn't in the cards.

It had been a week since I'd sent my rambling thoughts to Doozer and I'd heard nothing back. This didn't bode well for me, considering he was the communicator in our relationship.

"Trouble!" Taxi bellowed from outside my dorm room.

I pulled open the door with a huff. "What? You said we had the weekend off."

"You got a visitor."

"Who?"

"Follow me," he growled.

What fresh hell do you have in store for me now? I wondered as I slid on my shoes and stepped out of my room.

He scowled as we walked down the hall. "Let me be crystal clear. You still have the next forty-eight hours to yourself, but if you break curfew, I'm gonna fuckin' rain down so much pain on you, you'll wish you were dead."

"Wow," I breathed out as he stopped at the conference room door and pushed it open. "Who could possibly—"

"Hey, Steph."

I gasped as Doozer studied me from across the room. I heard the door close behind me and I rocked from foot-to-foot not sure what he was doing here.

"You gonna say hi?" he asked.

"Are you here to dump me?" I blurted.

He frowned. "I wasn't the one who wrote a Dear John letter. I'm here so you can tell me in person."

"I didn't write you a Dear John letter."

"What else would you call it?"

I bit my lip. "I was processing my thoughts. On paper. But I couldn't dump you if my life depended on it. Obviously."

He cocked his head. "Obviously?"

"Marco, I love you. I can't think straight because of it. Ergo, obviously."

He crossed his arms. "Your letter made it sound like you wanted to end things in order to think straight."

"I know," I breathed out. "I'd had no sleep and I was really sad. But ending things is not what I want on any level." I blinked in an effort not to cry. "I don't know what I'm trying to say, Doozer. You know I suck at this kind of shit."

His mouth twitched. "I do know that."

"And…?"

"Get your ass over here and kiss your man," he demanded, and I wrinkled my nose.

"*Or*… you can get *your* ass over here and kiss your woman."

He didn't hesitate, taking three long strides and wrapping his arms around me, lifting me off my feet. He kissed me so hard, I'm surprised we managed to stop ourselves from stripping down and fucking on the giant table.

"Fuck, baby, I missed you," he said after he broke the kiss.

"I missed you more."

"Doubtful."

"What are you doing here?" I asked once he set me on my feet. "Does Minus know?"

"That I'm here?"

"Yeah."

"He sent me."

I gripped his cut. "Shut the fuck up. Why the hell would Minus send you?"

He patted my butt. "Because I've been moping like a puppy who's just gotten swatted with a newspaper. He was over it."

I slid my hands up his chest. "I love you, honey. I'm sorry that letter was such a shitshow."

"Love you too. I'm very fuckin' glad the letter was a shitshow, rather than a fuck off."

"How long are you staying?"

"A few days. At least long enough to fuck you ten or twenty times."

I rolled my eyes. "One track mind."

"Look, if you want to talk and forgo my mouth on your pussy, I'm totally fine with that."

I shivered. "You have no idea how badly I want your mouth on my pussy."

"Taxi said the team's on furlough this weekend, is that right?"

"Yup," I confirmed.

"I've got a motel room close by. It's nothing fancy, but it's clean and it's private."

I grinned. "Then why are we standing here?"

"Good question, baby."

"I'll grab a couple of things from my room and meet you back here."

"Pack light, we'll be on a bike," he said.

"A bike? How did you manage that?"

"I made some calls before I got here and found out there's a Harley dealership that rents bikes near the airport. I figured you'd be jonesin' to get in the saddle by now. I thought we could go for a ride through the Virginia countryside tomorrow."

I gave Doozer the biggest kiss I could muster. "You are the best. I'll be back in five minutes."

"I'm timing you."

I let out a quiet squeak and rushed out of the room.

* * *

Doozer

Moments after Trouble left, Taxi entered the room, and he was rip shit pissed.

"I'm only gonna warn you once," he growled. "Take one step over the line while you're here and I'll send the both of you packing back to Portland."

"Look, I'm not here to fuck anyone's shit up, okay?"

"Why the hell are you here, Doozer?"

"I'm here for Trouble," I replied, calmly.

"Trouble is here to train."

"I understand that."

"If you did, you wouldn't be here."

"Look, Minus told me to—"

"I don't give a fuck what Minus said. This is my camp, and Trouble is my trainee, and I can't have her distracted."

"Trouble's also a member of the Burning Saints."

"Which will mean absolute dick when she's out in the field."

I laughed. "I thought you were smarter than that."

"What the fuck is that supposed to mean?"

"You may have recognized Trouble's talent with a rifle, but you have no idea what makes her tick."

"I suppose you have her all figured out," Taxi replied.

"I know she'll be thinking of her club when she's out running around with you. The only reason she's here is to protect the Saints."

"You're the one who doesn't understand. Trouble's here for her own reasons. She'd have come with or without Saints' blessing. She's more than just a biker, Doozer."

"You think I don't know that?" I snapped.

"Then leave her alone so I can help reach her full potential," Taxi shouted.

"Is *that* what this is?" Heat crept up the back of my neck. "You want to be alone with Trouble?"

Taxi's face dropped. "After all we've been through, I thought you'd have shown me a little more respect than that, Doozer."

"And I would have thought you'd respect our club's patch more. You'd be wise to remember that Trouble is only here because her president granted permission."

"Is that why Minus sent you? To remind me that he's the boss?" Taxi huffed.

"Did you come in here to remind me that *you're* the boss?"

"Something like that," Taxi replied, taking a step closer.

"If you're gonna get this close to me, you'd better be about to ask me to dance," I said through a steely gaze.

"This is your final warning, Doozer. Don't get in the way of Trouble's training, or you'll know firsthand what it's like to dance with me."

Trouble walked back in to find Taxi and me standing toe to toe.

"Lucky for you, my dance card is full right now," I growled only loud enough for him to hear, before turning away.

"Hey, Taxi," Trouble said. "Everything okay?"

"Great," he said. "Doozer and I were just catching up."

"Yup," I said, before turning to Trouble. "You ready?"

She nodded and said goodbye to Taxi, before leading us out the door.

* * *

Trouble

Doozer was quieter than normal as we made our way to his room. I wanted more than anything to know what he was thinking but was terrified to ask. And as curious as I may have been to crack into his skull, for the time being I had to admit I was more interested in what was in his pants. It's hard for me to explain, but sex with Doozer was unlike anything I'd experienced before. He didn't just take to me to heights of physical pleasure I'd never been before, but also to what I can only describe as a spiritual place. When we were having sex, nothing else in the world mattered. Not my past, or even my present. There was only the two of us.

As soon as we entered his room, I pushed Doozer down onto the bed and began quickly undressing him. My mouth hungrily kissing and licking every bit of his body that I exposed.

Once he was naked, I threw off my own clothes as quickly as I could, then jumped back on the bed. Straddling his hips, I guided him inside of me, closing my eyes as his girth filled me. I leaned down to kiss him and bit back tears at the thought of him leaving and not seeing those eyes every day. "I love you, Marco Mancini."

He kissed my neck, then ran his tongue over my pulse, burying himself deeper inside of me. "I love you too, Stephanie Palmer. That will never change."

"You don't have to make me promises, honey."

"And I don't say shit I don't mean," he countered, sliding a hand between us and fingering my clit.

Our physical connection in the past had always been frantic, lustful, passionate. And it wasn't as though it wasn't that now, it just happened to be slow and gentle as well. Doozer made love to me and we connected on a level much, much deeper than we ever had before. It was beautiful and terrifying all at the same time.

He rolled me onto my back and rocked into me slowly, kissing me as a climax built. "I can't wait," I rasped.

"I'm close, baby." He moved faster then. Slamming into me over and over until I could no longer hold back my orgasm, screaming his name as my walls contracted around him.

He wasn't far behind me, his cock pulsing as he came, then rolling us onto our sides facing each other.

"That was otherworldly," I whispered.

"Fuck, yeah it was." He chuckled, kissing me gently, then pulling out of me and stepping into the motel's tiny bathroom. He returned with a warm washcloth and cleaned me up, kissing me gently before pulling me back into his arms.

"Training can't be over soon enough," I complained.

"Agreed."

"What were you and Taxi talking about earlier?"

"Nothing important," Doozer said, unconvincingly.

"Really?" I challenged. "Because, it looked like some macho, he-man bullshit was going down between the two of you when I walked in."

"It's nothing," he said.

"Which means it was *something*."

Doozer sat up and faced me. "You didn't grow up with siblings, so you might not relate to this, but every Thanksgiving, the wishbone was a big deal in our house."

"The wishbone?" I chuckled, sitting up to face him, surprised by Doozer's left turn.

"Yeah, you know, the wishbone from the turkey."

"I know what a wishbone is, but what does this have to do with your conversation with Taxi?"

"When we were kids, my sisters and I would fight every year about which two of us got to pull the wishbone apart. It was supposed to be fun, but to us it was blood sport. A primitive ritual to find out which one of us would be bestowed with good luck for the year. Every year, no matter how good the meal was, or how well we'd be getting along all day, the moment that wishbone came out, it was war."

"I'm still lost," I said.

"I don't want you to be the wishbone in between me and Taxi," Doozer said, softly.

"Is that what was going on earlier? A game of tug of war with me as the prize?"

He sighed. "Yes and no."

"Okay, you need to start speaking 'Merican, buddy, because I'm about to lose my mind."

"I'm having a hard time letting go," he admitted. "I don't like that I'm being replaced—"

"You're not being replaced."

"Let me get this out. I need to verbally process."

"Sorry," I grumbled.

"I'm having a hard time letting go. Specifically, my need for you to need me… more than Taxi. I want to be the one to have your back. The one you need above all else, and the one who will protect you in any situation. But that's unrealistic. You have to trust your team, or it won't work, and I have to let you go enough not to interfere." He met my eyes. "Bottom line, I'm scared to death I'm gonna lose you. You're growing and learning at a breakneck pace, and I'm pretty sure you're gonna figure out just how much of a fuckin' loser I am."

"Hey, that's my man you're talking about," I growled.

He smiled slightly. "It's how I feel."

I squared my shoulders and nodded. "Anything else?"

"I think that pretty much covers it."

"Okay." I took his hand and ran my finger over his palm. "I love you. Not the kind of love that's gonna end tomorrow. The kind that lasts forever and since I know you're well aware I don't need a knight to slay my dragons for me, you protecting me doesn't factor into this. At least, within the little picture. In the bigger picture, obviously, I will expect you to always have my back and always protect me in all things because you're my man, and you're all fucking man which is one of the reasons I love you. And yes, I'm growing and learning, but honey, so are you. This conversation is evidence of that. You're saying out loud that you recognize you need to let me go and that's kind of remarkable, don't you think?"

"Well, I'm pretty fuckin' awesome, so…"

"You are." I laughed. "I'm not going anywhere. I'm going to finish my training, then regardless of if Taxi decides he wants to send me to Timbuktu, you're part of that package. He knows that. I've been clear about that, so it's a non-issue. The only reason it would be an issue is if you didn't want to come with me. And then, I'll be the one needing to figure out how to let you go." I let out a snort. "Who am I kidding? I'm never letting you go, so suck it up, buttercup, we're in this for the long haul."

"I'm not goin' anywhere, either."

"Good. Tell you what," I said. "The team is getting together for drinks tomorrow night at the Windmill. Why don't you come with me and you can meet everyone? Maybe if you meet the people who are gonna have my back, you'll feel a little better."

"Is Taxi gonna be there?"

"He said he might stop by briefly," I replied.

"*How* briefly?"

I smacked Doozer's chest. "He saved your life, remember?"

"Yeah, yeah. Why does everyone keep reminding me of that?"

"Because I, for one, am extremely grateful that he did."

He leaned forward and kissed me, and I cupped his face. "Feel like getting me dirty in the shower before getting me clean?"

"Hell yeah."

I grinned. "Race ya."

After our shower, I headed back to the barracks and slept better than I had in days.

Doozer

WE PULLED UP to the Windmill Bar and Grill just before ten o' clock and the place was packed. The spot looked like any average beer and wings joint you'd see in any college town, which was essentially what Quantico was. Except, instead of being populated by fresh-faced engineering and medical students, it was filled with fine young men and women learning new and better ways to kill people with their bare hands. Quantico itself is the size of a postage stamp, but houses high level training facilities for the

Marines, the Navy, the DEA, and of course the FBI.

We got off the rental bike and Trouble removed her helmet, her pixie-rocker hair, sticking out in every direction. However, with a shake of her head, and a quick comb through with her fingers her hair was once again picture perfect. It was like a magic trick.

"That why you keep your hair short?" I asked. "To avoid 'helmet head'?"

"No," Trouble replied. "For the longest time, my favorite movie to check out from the base library was G.I. Jane."

"With Demi Moore," I said.

Trouble's face lit up. "You've seen it?"

"Of course, I have. She's a total badass in that movie."

"Right?" Trouble asked, excitedly. "Well, after seeing that movie I became kind of obsessed with Demi Moore. *A lot* obsessed. Which led me to my all-time favorite movie, Ghost."

"You look like her, ya know?"

"Shut up!" she yelled, slapping my chest.

"What did I say wrong? Demi Moore is smokin' hot."

"Of course, she is," Trouble said. "Demi's the reason I cut my hair short. Because of how she wore it in Ghost. I would have done anything to look like her when I was a little girl."

"Well, you *do*."

"Stop saying that," she said, again playfully hitting at me.

"I'm serious," I repeated. "And you look beautiful tonight."

"I've been in civilian clothes for too long," she said. "I feel naked without my kutte."

"You wanna wear mine?" I asked.

"Yeah, right. It's only five times too big for me."

"Good, cause I kinda like seeing you dressed up for a night on the town."

"That's because you normally see me in a dirty pair of jeans and a t-shirt."

"Everything I see you wear becomes dirty in my mind."

"Shut up," she said, her cheeks now bright pink.

"How about you make me shut up," I said, leaning down for a kiss. Trouble's lips met mine and I pulled her close to me, my thumb going to her pulse. I deepened my kiss and Trouble moaned, loosening her grip on her helmet, causing it to fall to the ground with a loud crack. Not that we cared. My hand went to Trouble's ass, pulling her even closer, but before I could lean down for another kiss we were interrupted.

* * *

Trouble

"Excuse me. Hey! Is this guy bothering you?" a voice called out from behind us.

I turned to see Rabbit, Tackle, Jette, Boots, and Graves approaching us en masse and grinned. "Hey guys."

I introduced Doozer to the team, well, except Rabbit. They already knew each other, and bro hugged a little longer than most bikers typically did. As tough as my man was, he had a deep appreciation for his friends and never took them for granted. Whether he wanted to admit it or not, he was sweet, and I loved him for it.

"I need to drink," Jette said. "Especially since I'm not paying for any of it." She grinned at Boots and he sighed.

Boots was the Sergeant at Arms of the Bakersfield chapter of the Killing Jokers out of California. He knew everything there was to know about every type of firearm ever manufactured, but it seemed like his true joy in life was blowing things up. When he'd met Jette, he'd gone hard at her, making it clear that although he thought she was 'hot as fuck,' she couldn't possibly be smart enough to get one over on him.

Anjenette Smith, or 'Jette' as everyone called her, looked like Stevie Nicks circa 1972, and was pegged at eleven on the hippie scale. She was probably the smartest person I'd ever met and could hack anything anywhere. It was why she was here training with us. It was either that, or federal prison. Her brother, Rabbit, rode with the Dogs of Fire out of Savannah, and had also been roped into Taxi's schemes.

Boots had bet Jette that he had his personal data locked down 'tighter than a nun's asshole,' via the most sophisticated firewall software money could buy. He was certain, because he'd paid a moonlighting NSA security code writer to design it specifically for him, and she'd never be able to fuck with it.

Boots had been schooled, hard, by the petite hippie.

Jette had not only broken through his firewalls and protections, she'd done it in less than four minutes, her finger hovering over the keyboard with a grin before she dropped the digit on the enter button. "Done."

"Done, what?" Boots asked.

"I have just transferred all of your assets into an untraceable offshore account in the Caymans that may or may not be held by one of my many aliases."

"What the fuck?" he rasped, leaning down to look at her laptop screen.

"Hold on there, big man," she warned. "I could press this button and you could make a sizable charitable donation to the campaign to repeal the second

amendment of the Constitution."

"You fuckin'—"

"Jette," Rabbit warned, even though he'd been trying to hold back his laughter.

Jette raised an eyebrow in Boots' direction. "Drinks and mess duty for the rest of training and I'll put everything back where I found it."

"Yeah," Boots rushed out. "Whatever the fuck you want."

"Did you fill your wallet?" Jette asked Boots as we made our way to the entrance of the bar. "Because I'm getting shitfaced."

Boots rolled his eyes. "Since you've given my finances a colonoscopy, you obviously know everything I know, so try not to bankrupt me, yeah?"

She shrugged. "No promises."

There were two bouncers flanking the door, both as wide as they were tall, and looking every scary bit that their menacing jobs required.

We all grabbed our IDs, and Jette, Rabbit, and Boots made it through the door just as Doozer and I stepped up with Graves behind us.

Douchebag Bouncer Number One shook his head. "We sure as shit ain't lettin' scooter trash like you into the Windmill."

"What the fuck did you just say to me?" Doozer demanded, taking a step closer.

"I think you heard me just fuckin' fine, Yankee," he replied, spitting a wad of chew at our feet.

Doozer's right hand balled into a fist, but I grabbed it, holding it tightly in both of mine. "Doozer, no," I said softly. "I could get kicked out of the program."

"You should listen to your friend with the lesbo haircut," he said, smugly.

"Look," Doozer said, obviously trying his best to keep his shit together. "We didn't come here to fight. Sorry for any confusion. How about we all just go on about our own business."

The bouncer eyed me up and down. "You at Quantico?"

"Not really any of your fuckin' business," Doozer growled.

The bouncer pointed at me as he laughed with his counterpart. "Shit. How desperate is the FBI that they have to recruit dykes on bikes?"

I still had Doozer's right hand held tightly by my own, yet, he still managed to deliver a stiff jab with his left directly to the bouncer's nose, causing blood to gush instantly, all over his douchey designer shirt.

I let go and his buddy stepped toward us.

"No!" the leader yelled, waving him back. "He's mine."

"Apologize to the lady and I'll let you walk away now," Doozer said.

"You should be the one who's worried about walking away, boy," he said before lunging at Doozer wildly.

I stepped back as Doozer dropped as low as possible, using his shoulder to take him out at the knees. The bouncer's own forward momentum caused him to crash, face first onto the asphalt. Doozer then took his back and positioned him in choke hold. With his arm securely around his neck, tightly under his chin, it was clear to see Doozer was cutting off both his air supply and blood flow to his head.

"I told you, I don't want to fight," Doozer growled. "Tap out and apologize and we can all walk away—"

But the guy didn't have to tap out because out of nowhere, three guys rushed out of the building and then all of them were suddenly on Doozer, kicking and punching him.

"You fucking asshole," I bellowed, jumping on the back of one of their crew and biting down on his ear, causing him to shriek in pain as blood poured from the side of his head.

"Get her off me!" he screamed but I held on like a spider monkey, biting down harder until I'd managed to take a sizable chunk out of his ear, spitting the piece of his bloody flesh onto the pavement.

The rest of the crew froze momentarily, and Doozer managed to get back to his feet to square off with the leader once again.

"You made a big fuckin' mistake," he said, landing a right to his jaw, sending him to his ass.

Graves, who'd been outside with us, was holding his own with the bouncer's counterpart, while the rest of my crew was now outside assisting with the other assholes.

Doozer pounced on top of Douchebag Number One and grabbed him by the shirt collar before delivering two clean blows to the right side of his face, Doozer's rings carving chunks of flesh from the Bouncer's cheek.

I reached into my pocket and grabbed a pair of illegal brass knuckles, jumping into the fray with the rest of my crew. Fists and teeth flew until the inevitable sounds of police sirens broke up our little parking lot party.

Quantico's finest rolled up on us with lights flashing and all the colonial charm they could muster.

"Break it up and move away from one another," an officer's voice assertively, yet politely, requested over the car's loudspeaker. "Come on, Monty, Sean, Clifford. Let's go you guys."

Our opponents immediately complied to the officer's command. Stopping and standing in place as if they knew the drill. I took this time to deliver some justice for the earlier ambush on Doozer by driving my elbow directly into the bridge of my opponent's nose.

"Mother fucker," he shouted as blood began to pour from his face like a faucet.

"Now, come on. I asked you to break it up," the voice on the loudspeaker said, as if he was scolding a toddler. "Now, I want y'all to stand up, put your hands where I can see them, and get in a line."

The officers exited the car, guns and flashlights drawn, just as Taxi pulled up.

"Shit," I hissed, under my breath.

"I mean it, boys. Line up and stay real still," the first officer commanded.

"Those two are female, Sarge," the second officer said, pointing to me and Jette.

"What are you young ladies doing out here fighting in the Windmill parkin' lot?"

"I was about to ask the exact same thing, myself," Taxi said, approaching the officers with his shield and credentials in hand. "Good evening, Sergeant, my name is Agent Davis with the FBI. I work at the training facility and these young men and women are my cadets."

"Well, sir, your cadets have some explaining to do," the sergeant replied, before turning to the locals. "And so do you boys. Monty, Sean. All of you. I told you I didn't want to catch you boys out here fightin' anymore."

"We're bouncers. We're paid to fight," Monty said, through a mouthful of blood. "Besides, they started it."

"Given your track record, I find that unlikely," the sergeant said. "However, I don't have the room to hold all of you until we sort this out."

"I don't want to step on your toes, Sheriff, but if you'd agree to release my cadets into my custody, I can assure you they will be dealt with. Severely." Taxi glared at our motley crew.

"I think I'd be amiable to the idea, Agent Davis, but it doesn't rightly seem fair to lock these boys up while yours go free."

"It sounds like you know these boys pretty well," Taxi said.

"Yup," the Sergeant said with a heavy sigh as he pointed. "That one's my sister's kid."

"From the looks of it, these idiots seem to have taken their lumps pretty well, so maybe you let your guys go home and sleep it off and I'll get mine back where they belong. We'll agree to steer clear of the Windmill for the next ninety days when cooler heads can prevail. What do you say?"

"Sounds fair to me," the Sergeant replied. "How 'bout you boys?"

"I kinda need the money," Monty argued.

"You need a swift kick up the ass is what you need," his uncle countered. "Maybe Sonny can put you behind the bar. I'll talk to him."

The locals groaned in resignation.

"All right then, clear on outta here. Have Jerry call cars for y'all. Go home to your mamas and have 'em look at your bumps and bruises. Y'all don't be afraid to go to the emergency room if you have to."

"'Night uncle Bob," one of the crew called back to the sheriff.

I chuckled at the quaint small-town exchange and Taxi shot me a look that advised I'd be better off stowing my shit.

"Thank you, Sergeant," Taxi said, shaking the officer's hand. "I'll make sure my cadets get back to the barracks safely, but you can take this one with you," he said, pointing to Doozer.

"What the hell?" Doozer snapped.

"He's not with you?" the sergeant asked Taxi.

"He's not one of my cadets, and he's definitely not my responsibility."

"Well, we can certainly accommodate a party of one at our fine establishment," the Sheriff said, turning Doozer around to cuff him.

"Taxi, please don't do this," I begged.

"One more word, and you can join him," Taxi shot back, angrily.

"It's okay, Trouble," Doozer said in an assuring tone. "I'll be okay."

A knot formed in the pit of my stomach as I watched the officers stuff Doozer into the back of their cruiser and drive away.

Doozer

THE DOOR OF the holding cell slid open with a loud clang, waking me from my unsteady slumber.

"Mancini," the guard called out in an unnecessarily loud voice and I attempted to sit up, which proved to be a bad idea. My head felt like an overripened tomato and my body ached from the tap dance routine those boys did on me. I struggled to get out of my bunk as sharp pains shot through my ribcage.

"Mancini!" he yelled again, even louder.

"I'm right here, man," I responded, slowly rising to my feet, disoriented from pain and lack of sleep.

"You're free to go," he said, dryly.

"What?"

"Your lawyer is here. You're free to go," he said, waving me out of the cell.

"My lawyer?"

"You can pick up your belongings at processing. Come on, let's move it."

I followed the guard to the processing area, which was really the same desk I stood in front of when the officers brought me in last night. Behind the desk was a young male officer who looked to be straight out of the police academy.

"Marco Mancini for release," the guard said, barely pausing before returning the way we'd come.

"Good morning Mr. Mancini," the fresh-faced officer said cheerily.

"Um, good morning…I guess," I said, massaging my temples.

"If you would just sign this form, I can return your belongings, and get you out of here."

"Sure thing," I replied, scribbling something that vaguely resembled my signature on the form.

He then handed me a clear plastic bag containing my wallet, sunglasses, rings, and cell phone which had been shattered during last night's scuffle."

"Fuck me," I exclaimed. Trying in vain to get the phone to power on but it was no use. The thing was pulverized. "The guard said something about my lawyer?"

The desk officer pointed to a well-dressed man sitting on the bench directly behind me. He looked to be in his forties, with salt and pepper hair, carrying a briefcase, and wore expensive looking shoes.

"I don't know that guy," I said, loud enough for the

man to hear, and he stood, extending his hand for a shake.

"Carson Bird. I've been hired to act as your legal counsel."

"Hired by who?" I asked, ignoring his hand while I slid each ring onto its correct finger.

"I've been instructed to put you in contact with a third party before continuing," he said, pulling out his phone, dialing, and handing it to me.

I looked at the screen, but the contact info was blank. No matter, the mystery of who was on the other end would soon be solved.

I put the phone to my ear. "Hello?"

"Doozer?" Minus asked.

A pit formed in my stomach. "Yeah. It's me."

"Listen very carefully and don't say a goddamned word until I'm done. You're gonna get in a car with Bird and you're not gonna give him a single ounce of your shit. A private plane is waiting for both of you at Turner airfield. That plane will fly you to Savannah, where I will meet you in two days. Do you understand?"

I paused briefly before blurting out, "No. I don't understand at all. Savannah? Why am I going to Savannah so soon? I just got here to Virginia."

"And how long did it take for you to make a fucking mess there? You're gonna go to Savannah now because I told you to go to Savannah now. When you get there, Bird will take you to Double H."

"Double H?" I asked.

"It's Duke and Pearl's ranch. Bird is their lawyer. Duke's gonna put you to work for a few days until I get there. I'd tell you not to give him any crap either, but to tell you the truth, it'd be fun to see you try."

"A ranch? What am I supposed to tell Trouble? I can't even call her."

"Good," Minus snapped. "You two need to stay the hell away from each other. You hear me? Trouble has more important things to focus on than your jealous, drunken ass and I have to try and un-fuck everything you fucked last night."

"Minus, you don't know what happened—"

"Shut the hell up," he growled. "Trouble needs to focus on her training, and you need to follow orders by getting in that fucking car, and then on that fucking plane, right fucking now."

Minus hung up and I handed the phone back to the lawyer.

"Bird, huh?" I asked.

"You can call me Carson," he said, smiling.

"Doozer," I said, offering my hand this time.

He pointed to the door. "Shall we?"

Like the errant child I felt like, I led him outside, then followed him to the awaiting car.

* * *

Doozer

Our plane ride to Savannah was bumpy and the plane was cramped. I was sure Minus had intentionally booked the shittiest charter plane possible just to punish me. Fortunately for me and my aching head, the cops hadn't found Warthog's gummies inside my bag, which made the trip bearable.

We arrived at the Double H Ranch right at sunset. The oncoming darkness made it difficult to tell the full scope and size of the place, but from what I could make out, and judging by some of the properties we'd seen on the drive here, it appeared to be large. As we continued down the property's main road, Duke and Pearl's house came into view and it looked even more impressive than the ranch itself.

I let out a slow whistle. "Holy smokes, that's some setup."

"Five generations of Hills have lived in that house," Carson said. "And a Bird has always represented them."

"No shit? Have they always been in the horse trade?"

"Tobacco made the Hill family's original fortune. Then, after World War II, it was cattle. Once Duke's father died, Duke sold the cattle business and focused solely on breeding and training horses."

"Does he still do that now?" I asked.

"Duke keeps a small stable of horses, but at his age, it's getting tougher for him to put in a full day's work."

"Doesn't the ranch have employees?"

Carson grinned. "Sure, but Duke is what you'd call a hands-on kind of guy."

We reached the end of the long gravel driveway, parked, and got out of the car. An elderly couple sat together on the front porch of the house in matching rocking chairs.

"I'm surprised you remembered how to get to the ranch, it's been so goddamned long since you've been here," the old man called out as he rose.

"Hello, Duke. It's nice to see you too," Carson said, in a warm, but business-like tone.

"Did you have to use your GPS to find us?" Duke asked as he helped Pearl to her feet.

"Oh, Duke. You leave this nice young man alone," Pearl ordered, greeting Carson with a hug and a kiss on the cheek.

"Hello, Pearl. It's *genuinely* nice to see *you*," Carson said.

"See, that?" Duke shouted. "Goddamned lawyers. Always talking out of both sides of their mouths."

"I always thought that was a silly expression," Pearl

said. “Is it better for someone to speak only out of one side of their mouth? Would you really trust a person who spoke in such a way?”

“One side, both sides, it don’t rightly matter. Bird here is a lawyer, which automatically makes him an asshole and a liar.”

“Duke,” Pearl admonished.

“Granted, he’s not as big of an asshole as his daddy, and nowhere near the liar his granddaddy was, but he’s a lawyer and a Bird, so what the hell can he do?”

“I’ll remember this chat fondly while sending you my billable hours this month,” Carson said with a smile.

“I bet you will,” Duke said. His tone dripped with annoyance, but it was obvious Duke liked Carson Bird. “Well. You’re here, so you may as well come in for a drink,” Duke said before pointing at me. “Who’s this mopey looking sack of bruises you brought with you?”

“This is Doozer.”

“Nice to meet you, sir,” I said, shaking his hand.

“This is the queen of this here rodeo, Pearl,” Duke said, sweetly.

I nodded politely to Pearl. “Ma’am.”

“It’s very nice to meet you, Doozer,” Pearl replied. “Welcome to the Double H and please forgive my husband’s foolish rants. He is a good man, but he’s full of three kinds of bologna.”

“Doozer, huh? More like Doozy if you ask me,” he said, examining my bruises. “Looks like someone had themselves a square dance on your face, son.”

“Doozer ran into a little trouble with some local boys in Quantico,” Carson said.

“I thought Virginia was for lovers,” Duke said with a chuckle.

“Yeah, well I guess these guys didn’t get that message.”

"What about you?" Duke asked.

"What *about* me?"

"Did you get the message?"

"I don't know what you mean," I replied.

Duke put a hand on my shoulder and smiled. "Son, every ass-whoopin' is life's way of trying to deliver a message to you."

"Is that so?"

"Indeed, it is. So, let's go inside, rustle up some whiskey, and have us a chat. Maybe we can figure out exactly what life is trying to teach you."

"A drink sounds great," I said, still unsure about what he meant.

"Good," Duke said.

Duke led us up to the house and into his study, and Pearl excused herself for the evening. It was still way too early for bed, but I got the distinct impression she was retiring to leave the *men to their business*. Their whole vibe was old school as shit, and super cool to watch. Duke and Pearl were like something out of a movie. Their vibe reminded me of that scene in Godfather II when Michael Corleone meets with Hyman Roth in Florida. Hyman Roth's old lady brings him a tuna sandwich on a tray while he and Michael Corleone watch baseball and casually plot who's gonna get whacked.

"Scotch okay with you?" Duke asked, setting out three glasses.

"Whatever you're pouring, sir," I replied.

"Alright, you can knock off that sir shit. I'm a professional rancher and an amateur lover and neither of those things requires me to be addressed as sir. Duke'll do fine, son."

I nodded.

"So, Minus tells me you're a good kid, and a good

soldier," Duke said handing me my drink.

"I'm glad, if not a little surprised to hear that, but maybe club talk should stay between just you and me," I said, motioning toward Carson.

"I'm your lawyer, Doozer," Carson replied. "Whatever you say to me is confidential information bound by attorney client privilege."

"How exactly are you my lawyer? I don't have any money. I can't pay you," I said.

"I sent Bird to Virginia after Minus called me," Duke said, handing me my drink. "It was the least I could do, and I was happy to do it. Pearl and I owe our lives to Minus and Cricket."

"Who knows how long I would have rotted in the backwater shithole jail cell if you hadn't?"

"Let's just say, I've been in your boots before," Duke said with a grin before taking a slow sip.

"Minus said you were out in Quantico because of your woman. That right?"

I nodded. "She's enrolled at the FBI training academy."

"FBI training? A biker's old lady?"

"It's kind of a long story," I said, dismissively.

"You got anything better to talk about while we whack away at this here bottle?"

"I guess not," I laughed. Over the hour I brought Duke and Carson Bird up to speed. I told them all about Sweet Pea's standoff with Wolf, how the club had come to work with Taxi, and about Trouble joining his new team.

"Well, that Trouble sounds like a tough cookie," Duke said.

"She's amazing," I replied. "I've never met anyone else like her. Not even close."

"You love her?"

"Of course, she's perfect."

"You tell her that?"

I nodded, taking a sip.

"So, why don't you marry her?" Duke asked as plainly as possible.

"What?" I replied, almost spitting out my drink.

"Sure. You've been yapping away about her for an hour. You're obviously ass-over-brains in love with the girl. Why not make her your wife?"

"Make her my wife? What are we, back in the eighteen-hundreds?"

"I ain't that old, pecker head," Duke growled. "Young people are so goddamned touchy about marriage these days. Back in the day, if you loved a woman, you married her before she had the good sense to go off and find someone better."

"Relationships are a bit more complicated these days."

"You only think that because you're young and dumb. Do you really love Trouble?"

"Of course, I do, and I'm freaked the fuck out that she's gonna dump me now that she's starting this new life, but I don't think marriage is gonna solve anything."

"I didn't say it would," Duke said. "In fact, marriage doesn't solve anything. Ever. That's not what marriage is about."

"If getting married doesn't solve anything, then why encourage me to do it?"

"Because there's nothing more beautiful in this world than a kept promise."

"I don't follow."

"Look, son. Getting married is nothing more than two people who love each other making a promise between them. *Being* married is the daily fulfillment of that promise, and that, my boy, is where all the hard work is. It's also where you'll find the good stuff." Duke grinned wide through his bushy, grey beard.

"The good stuff, huh?"

"Oh, yeah. Trying to "out-love" each other every day. You can't go wrong with that, my boy."

"How do you "out-love" someone?"

"Most people think a relationship is a fifty-fifty kind of a deal. I give fifty, they give fifty, and together we've got one hundred percent. Right?"

"Sounds right," I said.

"Pig shit," Duke replied. "I say both sides have to give one hundred percent of themselves to the relationship for it to work. I give one hundred, and Pearl gives one hundred and together we get one hundred. I can't rightly explain how the math works, but after fifty or so years of marriage, I know that it does."

"Okay, but Trouble and I have been together for barley a year. It's a little early to be thinking about marriage."

"Is it?"

I cocked my head. "How long was it after you met Pearl that you knew you wanted to marry her?"

"The night we met, but in fairness, I didn't ask her until the next day."

"You asked Pearl to marry you the day after you met?"

"I suppose we knew each other back when we were little kids, but I'd forgotten about that."

"What did she say when you asked?"

"Whatta you think? She told me to buzz off. Thankfully, after much wooing, I convinced her to hitch her cart to my horse."

"So, how long did you date before you got married?"

"Four."

"What are you getting on my case for? Trouble and I

have only been together—"

"Days."

"What?" I asked, barely able to process what I'd heard.

"Pearl and I got married four days after getting reacquainted. Four and a half, technically speaking. She took a little convincing."

I looked over at Carson Bird, hoping for a little support from someone closer to my age, but he was out cold. Slumped down in the oversized leather chair, glass in hand, his mouth agape.

"He passed out half an hour ago. Those Birds are all a bunch of lightweights, but they make good lawyers."

"Seriously, though, Duke. What am I gonna do about the cops back in Virginia?"

"You let me and Bird take care of that. Between his lawyerin' and my checkbook, I 'xpect we'll have everything cleared up by the time Minus gets here."

"Don't remind me," I groaned. "My old man, Taxi, Trouble, and now Minus. Who else's shit list could I possibly get myself onto?"

"Don't worry. We're gonna keep you so busy, you won't have time to think about your troubles. If you'll forgive the pun," Duke said, tipping his imaginary cowboy hat.

* * *

Trouble

"Nineteen!" Taxi shouted and I braced myself for the oncoming deluge. The blast of cold water stung against my aching back and my teeth chattered uncontrollably as I struggled to complete my next pushup. After a few seconds, Taxi continued. "Twenty," he called out before unloading the hose on the group once again.

So far, our punishment had consisted of sleep deprivation, a ten-mile hike, breakfast KP, and now pushups while being pummeled by a firehose.

"I told you that fighting would not be tolerated, didn't I?"

"Sir. Yes, sir," we shouted in not-so-perfect unison. Earning us another blast from the hose.

"What?"

"Sir. Yes, sir!"

"Attention," Taxi commanded, and we struggled to snap to our feet.

In all my years on the road, I'd never been more exhausted, cold, or hungry. I was soaked to the bone and seeing double.

"When I say no fighting, that means absolutely no fucking fighting. Not with each other and most definitely, not with civilians," Taxi walked down the line, addressing each of us as he passed. "In fact, the only thing you should be fighting is the urge to fuck up again. Because, if any of you behave like this once more, you'll look back on the last twenty-four hours with fondness. Have I made myself perfectly clear?"

"Sir. Yes, sir!"

"Good. There's chow waiting for you back at the dorms. Shower, eat, and rest. In that order. Get warm. Training will resume at thirteen hundred hours. Dismissed and get the fuck out of my sight."

I made my way to the barracks as quickly as my battered body would allow. I was nearly delirious from hunger, but my impending frostbite urged me back to my room, and I stepped into a hot shower, reveling in the warmth until my stomach couldn't take the emptiness anymore.

I couldn't wait to devour food. Any food. That was until I discovered with horror the breakfast Taxi had arranged for us.

He'd put a folding table right outside the barracks, and on top he'd placed several stacks of MREs, courtesy of the US Department of Defense. MREs or meal-ready-to-eat are the pre-packaged staple of all deployed military personnel. The meals consist of a nutrient dense main course, side dish and dessert all contained in a single pouch. Anyone who's had to eat them will tell you that most MREs are barely tolerable. The selection Taxi laid out for us was simply diabolical.

"Holy shit," Boots said, looking through the packets. "There's only shit like Veggie Burgers and Beef Enchiladas here."

"No chili mac?" Tackle asked.

"Chicken Fajitas don't sound too bad," Graves said, holding up a package.

"That's because you've never had them," Boots said.

"Holy shit. Veggie omelet," Tackle said. "They Don't even make this one anymore. Where the hell did Taxi find these?"

"Yo. I think that shit is against the Geneva Convention," Boots said.

"How do you two know so much about MREs? Were you in the service?" I asked.

"Marines," Tackle said, motioning to Boots.

"Oorah!" Boots called out without pausing his search for the best meal in the pile.

"What about you?" I asked Tackle.

"No, not me. I'm an MRE connoisseur because of my dad."

"He in the military?"

"Not anymore. More like the militia."

"Gotcha," I said, figuring the fewer questions, the better.

"I knew he was pissed, but not this pissed," Boots said, tossing an MRE back on the pile. "Screw this. I'm hitting the rack."

As good as sleep sounded, I had to eat something, so I decided on the Veggie Burger.

Eight hours later I would learn, first-hand, how MRE got the nickname "Meals Refusing to Exit."

After the worst breakfast ever, I laid down in my bunk and tried to sleep. Even though I was exhausted beyond measure it took a little while for me to fall into a deep sleep as my brain was bombarded with thoughts of Doozer.

Doozer

EVERY MOVIE AND cartoon ever made would have you believe that a rooster's crow happens at the precise moment the sun rises over the horizon. Signaling the optimal moment for those on the farm to rise and greet the day. Hollywood always depicts the rooster standing high atop the barn, next to a weathervane, proudly trumpeting the arrival of the new day, no more than a total of two or three times, while being accompanied by an uplifting score of strings and flutes. This is, as Duke might put it, ten pounds of pig shit stuffed into a five-pound sack.

My feathered nemesis began his assault on my slumber around four thirty A.M., well before sunrise, and didn't stop until sometime around two P.M. I swear to Christ, I heard that little pecker cock-a-fucking-doodling all day long. It is also noteworthy that he didn't crow from atop the barn, but instead preferred to deliver his early morning serenade from directly outside the window of my first-floor room.

By five fifteen, I'd abandoned all hope of falling back to sleep. I got up, got dressed, and made my way to the kitchen in hopes of rustling up some coffee. I was surprised to find Pearl already there, decked out in an apron, preparing a full breakfast.

"Oh, dear. Did I wake you, sweetie? Or are you an early riser like me?" Pearl asked.

"Neither." I replied, pointing a thumb back towards my room. "The rooster outside my window told me it was time to get up."

"Oh, that would be Roger," she said, before flipping a pancake with expert precision. "He's a nasty one. I swear he's going to end up in my frying pan one of these days if he keeps up his nonsense."

I laughed. My eyes transfixed on Pearl's griddle. "Are those blueberry pancakes?" I asked.

"Yes, they are, and I'll have a warm stack for you ready in no time. If you'd like coffee, please help yourself to the pot. Mugs are in the cupboard to the right of the sink."

"I woke up to the chicken from hell but now find myself in heaven," I said and poured myself a cup of Pearl's house blend.

"It sounds like Duke's got a full day planned for the two of you, and I never like my boys to go to work on an empty stomach."

"Full day of work?" I asked, just as Duke entered the kitchen.

"Y'ain't afraid of a little hard work are ya, Doozer?" he asked, before greeting his wife with a kiss.

"No, sir. But I am gonna need more of this," I said, raising my mug.

"Is last night's scotch fightin' back this mornin'?"

"Roger started in a little early this morning," Pearl informed Duke.

"I'm so used to his racket, I don't even hear that old sonofabitch anymore," Duke said.

"You can't hear anything anymore, you old coot," Pearl said under her breath.

"And just because I didn't hear what you said, doesn't mean I don't know you said it, woman," Duke called out, taking his seat at the breakfast table.

I poured myself a second cup and joined Duke at the table.

"You ever branded a foal before, Doozer?"

"I'm not even sure what a foal is," I replied.

"That's a baby horse, son."

"The only branding I've ever seen was…well, never mind," I replied, flashing back to Clutch's short-lived patch-out party.

"Well, you're gonna learn a few things today. I've got a half dozen foals that are ready to be weaned from their mothers and moved out to pasture. Before I can do that, I've gotta get 'em branded and I can't do it by myself. Chako, my lead ranch hand has the day off but now that you're here I figured you could help me."

"Whatever you need," I replied, trying to hide the terror in my voice. Unlike Minus, who was as comfortable on a horse as he was a bike, I had zero experience with livestock and generally tended to stay away from anything with teeth larger than mine. Not to mention I was still pretty banged up from the bar fight.

"That's the spirit," Duke said, grinning wide through his whiskers.

Pearl arrived at the breakfast table with a stack of hot pancakes, homemade syrup and butter from their local farmers' market that was almost better than sex. Conversation around the table was easy and the food was out of this world. It was one of the best breakfasts I'd ever had, but with each bite I found myself wishing Trouble was here with me.

We cleared the table and helped clean up before heading out to the section of the pasture where the foals and their mothers were kept. Duke drove us in what looked like a post-apocalyptic cross between a golf cart and a flatbed truck. It sported flood lights, a winch, all terrain tires, and was murdered out in matte black.

"I call her Maxine. As in Mad Maxine. She's electric," Duke said proudly as we climbed inside.

"Looks like a fun ride," I said, noting the vehicle's roll cage.

"I needed something sturdy to get around in, and I'm too damned old to ride my bike anymore so I had Chako build me this souped-up baby. I figured why not have a little fun while I'm doing my chores?"

No sooner had the words passed through Duke's moustache, when he pressed the pedal to the metal and we went screaming down the dirt trail leading to the pasture.

"She's got a lot of pickup," I replied, and hung on for dear life.

Duke roared with laughter as we tore down the trail at breakneck speeds, slowing down only as we approached the herd.

"Don't wanna scare our equine friends," Duke said, rolling to a gentle stop near the pasture.

The ranch was even more spectacular than I had imagined. Sprawling green hills dotted with groves of mature trees stretched on as far as the eye could see in every direction. The air was crisp, and the morning sun painted the sky with a vibrant orange hue.

We climbed out of Maxine and Duke lead us to the pasture's gate. About a dozen horses, stood together in a fenced in area, casually munching on grass, completely unphased by our presence.

"Is this all of your herd?"

Duke laughed. "No, these are just the mamas and their foals. The mature herd is in the north pasture and our personal horses are in the stables. I'll take you up there later for an introduction."

"Sounds…good," I said.

"What's the matter, son?" Duke asked, noticing my hesitation. "Y'aint afraid of horses are ya?"

"To tell you the truth, I haven't been around them much. At all, really."

"Don't they have horses up there in Oregon?"

"I grew up in the suburbs, so the only horses I saw were at the Rose Parade or the fair."

"Well, these here animals ain't nothin' to be afraid of, but they should always be treated with the respect and an understanding that they can kill you."

"Nothing to be afraid of. Check." I said, giving Duke a thumb's up.

Duke chuckled. "What I mean is, these horses are broken and used to people, but there are rules to follow, and as long as you do, you and the horses will be safe."

"Okay," I edged out.

"Except for that one there," he said, pointing to a large black and white horse. "That's Bubba."

"Is he the king stud or something?" I asked.

"Well, ya see, ya might not know it by lookin' at

’em, but horses are very social animals. And some horses get sorta attached to other horses. Not necessarily a breeding pair, mind you. Just a bond between two animals that makes ’em easier to deal with as a pair rather than alone. Bubba and Penny over there have just such an arrangement. If Bubba is around, Penny is calm.”

“Your horse has an emotional support horse?”

“I guess you could say that,” Duke said with a chuckle.

“Carson said this used to be a cattle ranch.”

“That’s right. But the Double H has been in the horse racket since my daddy died and me and Pearl took over the place. I still keep a small head of cattle for milk, beef, and the occasional trade or sale. And as much as I’d hate to admit it, a little bit for old time’s sake. Like ol’ Hank Junior said, ‘It’s a family tradition,’” Duke sang out.

“Why the change? Is there more money in horses than cattle?”

“Shit no,” Duke laughed. “But I guess you could say that I didn’t have much interest in following in my daddy’s bootsteps.”

“I get that,” I said.

“I take it your daddy isn’t in an MC?”

I chuckled. “Not exactly. He’s a lawyer. Or *was* a lawyer until last year when he retired.”

“A lawyer?” Duke exclaimed.

“My sisters, and my uncle too. Pretty much, everyone except me.”

“I threw hell at Bird all night about being a lawyer within a family of lawyers, and you didn’t say nothin’ the whole time.”

“You think I was gonna sign up to face that firing squad?”

“Smart kid,” Duke replied with a tip to his trucker

cap.

"Plus, like I said. I'm not looking to follow my father's path any more than you."

"How 'bout you help me get the branding gear out of the back of Maxine and you can fill me in on the path you *are* on."

Even though Duke was virtually a stranger to me, I found him easy to talk to, even about the personal stuff I didn't talk to anybody about.

"Can I ask you a question first?"

"So long as you understand I have a fifty-fifty chance of being full of more horse shit than that pasture over there," Duke said, motioning to the herd.

"I don't mean any disrespect, or to sound like I'm ungrateful for your hospitality, but you seem to care a lot about someone you just met. What's up with that?"

"What do you mean?"

"I don't know. I guess I'm just not used to people I don't know asking me questions. You and Pearl seem really nice and Minus speaks highly of you, so I guess I'm just trying to figure out what the hell I'm doing here."

"I didn't mean to pry, it's just that when a Saint shows up on my door it's for a reason. From what I understand you won't be staying with us for long, so I suppose I'm trying to figure out why the hell you're here as well." Duke laughed heartily, throwing him into a coughing fit.

"You okay?" I asked as Duke struggled to catch his breath.

"I'll be alright," Duke said, regaining his composure. "I'll tell you, son. This gettin' old thing is for the birds," he said, motioning to the back of Maxine. "Help me get the gear out, will ya."

Duke dropped Maxine's tailgate, revealing a folding

table with two chairs, and a black medical bag.

"Is this all of it?" I asked, expecting to see an array of branding gear.

"Everything we need is right in here," he said, picking up the bag. "Grab the rest, will ya?"

"Where are the irons and the torch?"

"I haven't taken a brand to a horse in twenty years," Duke replied.

"But you said—"

"I still call it branding, because "chipping" a horse sounds stupid coming outta my mouth."

Duke opened the bag to reveal syringes, hair clippers, a deck of playing cards, and several bottles.

"One of them bottles is for the horses… and one's for us," Duke whispered like a little kid with a secret.

"What is all this?" I asked.

"Branding takes several hours, and four guys to do it. Plus, it don't make the horses very happy."

"I can't imagine it does," I said."

"Instead, I chip my horses. Then, I use all the time I saved to play cards and day drink." Duke held up the bag. "There's six syringes in here. Each one has a microchip in it. All we gotta do is shave off a patch of hair on their necks, give em a quick scrub with what's inside bottle number one, inject a chip into each one of 'em, and then it's onto those cards and what's in bottle number two. Whatta ya say?"

"Sounds a lot better than what I was expecting," I said, breathing a sigh of relief that wrestling livestock to the ground wasn't in my future.

"Let's get set up over there by the fence line," Duke said, and guided us to the spot that would become our "branding station."

Duke shoved his fingers in his mouth and let out a loud whistle and within seconds, I saw Bubba trot up over the hill with a whinny. Penny wasn't far behind, and her baby was following as close as it could.

"Wow," I said.

"He knows my call," Duke explained as the horse slowed to a walk and lumbered toward him. Duke handed him a carrot and stroked his nose, crooning softly to him.

Before long, a wild herd of beasts came running, kicking up dust behind them, and I couldn't stop myself from stepping back as they surrounded Duke.

"You can't show fear," Duke said, grabbing my shoulder to keep me next to him.

I notice Bubba pin his ears back and move to bite another black and white horse getting a little too close for comfort.

"Bubba, you leave Goliath alone," Duke ordered, as Bubba made a cricket sound in the back of his throat.

"Is he protecting his kid?" I asked.

"Oh, Bubba's not the sire. And that there's a filly. Girl foal." Duke pointed to Penny's baby, now suckling at her mama's teats. "Bubba's a gelding, so we bred Penny with Dumbass."

"You named a horse Dumbass?"

"Considerin' he's a dumbass, I sure did. But that horse is fast and pretty, so is Penny, so we're hopin' their foal'll do somethin' great." He grinned. "She's one of the ones we're gonna chip."

I looked at the tiny horse and nodded. "She doesn't look so tough."

Duke laughed, grabbing a rope, and throwing it over one of the bigger horse's necks. "Hand me those clippers."

He showed me how to do the process on three horses, before handing me the 'lead' and nodding to Penny's filly. "Your turn."

I approached the horse as Penny watched me warily, throwing the rope over the filly's neck and securing it the way Duke had done. Well, I tried to. The horse let out a squeal turning quickly and kicking her hind feet out, delivering a direct hit to my ribs.

I couldn't stop a groan as I fell flat on my ass, my lungs devoid of air while Duke let out a bellow of laughter as the horses all made a run for it… as far away as they could get from me.

"Fuck," I hissed, pulling my cut away from my body and lifting my shirt. "If I hadn't been wearing my leather, that little bitch coulda broken my ribs."

Duke grinned, holding a hand out to me and helping me to my feet. "I knew that little girl was gonna do somethin' great."

I scowled as I pressed a hand against my side and tried to catch my breath. "How the hell are we gonna get her back?"

"Give it a minute," he said, setting up the card table and two chairs. "Take a seat."

I gladly fell onto the metal folding chair and downed the glass of bourbon he'd set in front of me. Duke let out another whistle and then sat down and waited for Bubba and Penny to make their way over the hill again. Penny looked at me like she wanted to kill me, but maybe I was projecting.

"Are we gonna try again?" I asked.

"*We* ain't doin' nothin'. You're gonna keep your ass in your seat and let a professional handle it."

I didn't argue as Duke made quick work of chipping the filly.

"Okay, brother, you gotta name her," Duke said, once he was done.

"Name who?"

"The filly. You were her first kick, so you get the

honor."

I chuckled. "Well, since there's only one other woman who's kicked me close to my heart without killing me, I'm gonna name her after her. Trouble."

Duke grinned. "I think that's entirely appropriate." He released Trouble's lead and she trotted back to her mother as Duke joined me at the table again.

We drank until the sun started to set, then Duke drove us back to the house where Pearl had prepared enough food to feed an army. Despite the pain in my ribs, I ate until I nearly exploded, falling into bed, happier than I'd been in a while.

All-in-all, the day ended better than it had started. Little did I know, my happiness was going to be short lived.

* * *

A pounding on my door pulled me from my sex dream about Trouble and I snapped out, "What?" as I forced my eyes open.

"Call for you," Duke called through the door.

I glanced at the clock beside the mattress. One A.M.

Groaning, I slid gingerly off the bed and dragged on sweats before pulling open the door. "Who the fuck's callin' me at one in the mornin'?"

"Minus," Duke said. "He's on the land line. Phone's in the kitchen."

"Okay," I rasped. I needed to get a new phone, stat. I headed to the kitchen and picked up the receiver. "Minus?"

"You need to come home. Right now," he said.

"What's going on. I thought you needed me to go to Savannah?"

"I'm sending Tacky instead," Minus replied, in a low tone. "You need to come home, Doozer. It's your father."

My heart sunk. "What's wrong?"

"He's in the ICU at Legacy. He was attacked but we got to him before they could…do anything worse."

"Attacked? By who? And what do you mean *we* got to him? Minus, what the fuck is going on?"

"Just get home, kid," he said softly. "I sent a car to take you to the airport. It should be there soon. I'll be at the hospital when you get here."

"Fuck, fuck, fuck," I hissed out once I'd hung up the phone.

Heading back to my room, I packed my bag, shoving my boots on just as the car arrived.

Duke was standing on the front porch smoking a cigarette and he faced me as I started down the steps. "You let Pearl know when you get back safe, ya hear?"

I smiled. "Yeah, brother, I'll let *Pearl* know."

Duke gave me a chin lift and I climbed into the car, dreading the shitstorm I was about to go home to.

Fuck me and the horse I rode in on… or got kicked by… or whatever the fuck old-tyme adage worked in this situation.

Trouble

I WALKED INTO Dr. Fenton's office this morning looking forward to our session. It had been four days since our last one, and I was in serious need of her counsel. Since the last time I'd seen her, I'd managed to earn three black eyes. One on my face, and two on my cadet record. After my back-to-back failures, I was confident Taxi was going to tell me to pack my bag and I hoped Dr. Fenton would have some insight on how I could persuade him to reconsider. Or maybe I could just ask him myself.

I entered to find Taxi sitting in the center of the room next to an empty chair and Dr. Fenton seated behind her desk.

"Good morning," Dr. Fenton said, cheerily. "I've asked Taxi to join us for today's session."

"I can see that," I replied, not so cheerily.

"I know this time is typically reserved for just the two of us to talk, but I thought now might be a good time for the three of us to have a chat," Dr. Fenton said.

"A chat?" I asked, as my insides twisted into a knot. I began to ramble nervously. "Look, if you guys are gonna kick me out of the program please just tell me now because I'd rather not draw this out any longer than we have to—"

"Trouble," Dr. Fenton, said sweetly interrupting me. "Please, take a seat."

I did as she asked, avoiding eye contact with Taxi as I did. I couldn't believe that after all I'd been through, I was about to wash out.

"Taxi, would you like to start us off?" Dr. Fenton asked.

"Sure," he said, turning to me. "Trouble, why are you here at Quantico?"

"What are you talking about?" I asked, taken aback by his question. "I'm here because you asked me to be here."

"Just because I recruited you, doesn't mean you had to say yes. What I'm asking is, what made you accept my invitation to come here?"

I twisted in my seat, desperately searching for the answer Taxi was looking for.

"I guess I didn't realize I was being recruited. I just thought you had taken an interest in my shooting ability and one thing led to another."

"You think I asked you to join an elite undercover

FBI team because I took an interest in your shooting ability?" he asked.

"*Yes,*" I hissed.

Taxi paused for a moment before asking, "Trouble, do you remember the night we met?"

"It would be a little hard to forget," I replied.

"I remember it, too. Quite clearly," Taxi said, warmly. "When I met you, I felt like I'd found a diamond in the rough. I may have stumbled upon you with a rifle in your hand, but I had no idea if you could use it or not. As a matter of fact, if I recall correctly, you were set up to miss the shot that I interrupted."

"Is that why you're sending me home? Because I'm not a good enough shot?"

"Not good enough?" Taxi asked, sounding genuinely shocked. "Trouble, that double kill in Hogan's Alley was like nothing I'd ever seen. Like nothing any of the trainers here have seen. It's all everyone is talking about."

"What? But you said we failed. You said *I* failed."

"Tactically, you may have made the wrong call, but that shot was one in a million. Or two in a million, I don't know, but the point is, you're an even better shot than I thought you'd be. The question is, can you be the *agent* I need you to be?"

"Why did you choose to engage?" Dr. Fenton asked.

"Three of my team members were in immediate danger," I said.

"And you believed this enough to defy the engagement protocols of the mission?" Taxi asked.

"Yes, sir."

Taxi paused. "And I'd be willing to bet you'd make the same call if given the chance to do it all over again."

"I'm not gonna lie," I breathed out. "I would."

"I see," Taxi said.

"Maybe I've been in an MC for too long, or maybe I'm just not good agent material, but I'd break every rule in the FBI handbook to keep my brothers and sisters safe."

"Well, I guess that's everything I need to hear," Taxi said plainly, before rising to his feet and extending his hand to me.

My heart felt like a tin can being crushed under the weight of disappointment and my knees weakened as I stood to shake Taxi's hand.

"I'm going to need you to return to the barracks and pack your gear," Taxi said.

I nodded, managing to fight back the tears as Taxi continued.

"And make sure you don't forget anything, because you'll be staying in the senior dorms for the last two weeks of your training."

My head snapped to meet Taxi's eyes. "What?" I asked, unsure if I'd heard him correctly.

"Welcome to the team," Taxi said.

"But, you said—"

"Trouble, if you think I recruited you because I thought you'd shut up and do as you were told, or even because you're a great shot, you're not only wrong, but you're selling yourself short. I need you on this team because you fight for the people you care about. That's what I see in you and that's the kind of person I want on my team."

"Are you fucking kidding me?" I hugged Taxi so hard I thought I might break his spine, and this time I was unable to hold back the tears.

Taxi laughed, patting my back before setting me away from him. "I'm going to let you two finish your session."

Without another word, he walked out the door and I

faced Dr. Fenton.

She waved me back to my seat, then sat on the edge of her desk and grabbed the box of tissues she always kept there, handing it to me.

I ripped four out of the box as I burst into even uglier tears. Dr. Fenton left her spot on the desk, pulling a chair up beside me close enough to wrap her arm tentatively around my shoulders. "I am so proud of you, Trouble."

I let out an inelegant snort. "Oh, yeah, I'm a right winner, bawling my eyes out and filling your tissues with snot."

"You're knocking down your walls and letting people in," she countered. "The crying's just a bonus. The body letting off steam, so to speak. You would have never showed this to me at the beginning. You've embraced the work, sweetie, and not only is Taxi proud of you, but I am as well. Well done."

This only made me cry harder, which in turn, sent me into a fit of giggles. Jesus, I was bi-polar. This whole thing was making me crazy.

But it had also started to heal me in a weird way. The people I was letting in were guarding my heart and letting me be totally me. I trusted them and I didn't think I'd ever get to this place.

"Thanks for all your help," I rasped.

"Oh, this was all you, honey," Dr. Fenton countered. "I just asked you a few questions, but you did the work." She gave my shoulder a squeeze. "You have graduated my program, which means, unless you want to, you don't have to see me again, at least for this portion. I'll still be part of your briefing and debriefing protocol, but that will be on a per-mission basis."

I met her eyes. "Really?"

She grinned, nodding her head. "Really."

"Wow." I sniffed, wiping my eyes. "That's…um, wow."

She stood. "Right, it's time for you to go pack, so how about you do that now, so you don't have to see me blubber like a baby." She snagged an envelope off her desk. "But first, here's your phone back. You're free to use it at will."

I stood, unable to stop myself from pulling her in for a hug. "Thanks for everything."

"Anytime."

I escaped the emotion and headed back to my room, packing up and moving quickly into senior housing amazed I'd made it. I texted Doozer and let him know the good news, then met my team in the mess hall to celebrate.

Doozer

BY THE TIME I'd arrived at Legacy hospital, my father was out of the ICU and had been moved into a private recovery suite. After spending some time with Mama and my sisters, I checked in with Minus and Sweet Pea, who'd stayed at the hospital with my family all through the night.

"Thank you both for being here. It means a lot to me," I said.

"Some of the other guys and the old ladies were here last night too," Minus said.

"I'll be sure to thank 'em.'

"Any news?" Sweet Pea asked.

"He's pretty banged up, but the doctors were able to stop the swelling in his brain and it looks like there won't be any permanent damage. He's resting now and the nurse said I can go in and see him once he wakes up."

"Glad to hear it," Minus said.

"What the hell happened?" I asked. "Did the Beast do this?"

"It was the judge, man," Sweet Pea replied.

"Judge Snodgrass?"

The two men nodded in unison.

"The day after you spoke with your old man, he went to the judge to tell him the deal was off. Apparently, they belong to the same country club, and your father figured it would be safest to meet in a public place where the judge would be less likely to flip out."

"He was wrong," Sweet Pea said.

Minus continued, "The two of them were having lunch together when at some point, the judge started chasing your father around the dining room, screaming at the top of his lungs."

"We figure that's when your father broke the news."

"Eventually Snodgrass chased your father all the way to the pro shop, where he picked up a golf club and attacked your father."

"A golf club?" I asked.

"Sand wedge," Sweat Pea said.

"How do you know all of this?"

"The night you spoke with your father, I put Spike on protective duty."

"You put a tail on my father?"

"I figured the Beast wouldn't be happy about your father breaking his deal and wanted to make sure he was protected in case they tried to retaliate."

"Looks like the judge got to him first," Sweet Pea said.

Minus sighed. "Spike would have jumped in sooner, but the country club staff wouldn't let him inside the dining room. He was waiting outside when the judge went off, and by the time Spike got to him, the judge had already given your father a couple of solid whacks to the head."

"Did the cops arrest Snodgrass?" I asked.

Minus nodded. "Yeah."

"So, he's in jail?"

Minus and Sweet Pea looked at each other.

"You've gotta be fucking kidding me," I said.

Sweet Pea grimaced. "He's a judge, man."

"Who attacked another man with a golf club in the middle of a pro shop," I pointed out.

"He was out on bail before your father was even out of surgery."

"That motherfucker," I seethed.

"Well, your old man is safe now," Minus said.

"Thanks to all of you," I said.

"We're family," Minus said. "We look out for each other."

"You didn't have to look out for him, and you did anyway."

"You and your old man may have your differences, but he's your family, so he's our family too."

"Mr. Mancini," a nurse said. "Your father is awake and is asking for you."

I nodded and headed into the room. My mother hugged me and then smoothed her palms over my kutte. "I'm going to take the girls to the chapel. Light a candle and pray."

"Okay, Mama," I said, and my family left me with

my father who patted the mattress.

I pulled a chair up to his bed and smiled. "You got the presidential suite I see."

I'd never seen a hospital room so fancy, complete with private balcony. Not that it did much for a view today, considering, in pure Pacific Northwest fashion, it was pissing down with rain. I often forgot just how much money my parents had, mostly because I saw money as a curse the majority of the time. But when you're sick, it was certainly a good thing.

Dad nodded. "I'm sorry, son," he rasped.

"It's okay, Pop, you just get better."

"I should have listened to you."

"Let's not worry about that right now," I said.

"I was wrong about you and I was wrong about…your club. They saved my life," Pop said, then let out a groan.

"Shit. You in a lot of pain?"

He nodded and I shot out of my seat, heading straight for the nurse's desk down the hall.

"Can I help you, Mr. Mancini?"

"My father's in pain, can you give him something? He's in room 2112."

"I'll check his chart and be right in."

I nodded, rushing back to Pop's room, and stepping inside. "Okay, Pop, I found a nurse and she's gonna bring you some—"

I entered the room to see Judge Snodgrass holding a pillow over my father's face. Pop's body writhing as he struggled to breathe.

"Hey!" I yelled, causing the judge to drop the pillow and retreat towards the balcony.

Knowing Judge Snodgrass had no place to escape, I checked on my father who was coughing but breathing.

"You okay?" I asked and he gave me a quick head

nod just as Minus and Sweet Pea came bursting into the room.

"Stay with my father!" I yelled to Minus.

"I'll get security," Sweet Pea said, and rushed out of the room.

I quickly turned to see the judge climbing over the balcony railing. I have no idea where the fucker thought he was going. We were twenty stories up and the last I checked, judges couldn't fly.

By the time I reached him, Judge Snodgrass had swung both legs over the railing and was making his way to the east side of the balcony. The judge was a former collegiate track and field champ and even competed with Steve Prefontaine at the University of Oregon back in the day. For a man in his early seventies, he was fit as hell.

"Where the fuck are you going?" I called out as Spider-Judge continued to inch along the outside railing.

"She'll kill me," Judge Snodgrass yelled. "You don't understand."

I peered over the edge and could now see that the judge was headed for the balcony of the room next door.

"You'll never make it," I called to him. "It's too far to jump."

"I'll take my chances," he replied, continuing his futile escape.

"You're gonna fall."

"Better than what she'll do to me," Snodgrass said.

"Who are you talking about? Who's going to kill you?

"Your father ruined it all," the judge cried out. "I was gonna make him rich and that self-righteous son of a bitch blew it. Now I'm a dead man."

"Wrong," I said. "You're going to jail, and I'm gonna make sure of it."

He shook his head. "Not a chance. You know what they'll do to a judge in prison?"

"You're never gonna make that jump, so why don't you let me help you get back over the rail and we can let the police handle the rest."

The judge laughed. "This isn't just about me, you know. Daphne's coming for you. For your club."

"Who the fuck is Daphne? Are you talking about the Beast?"

"Daphne is just part of the black, twisted heart of the Beast," he replied, truly seeming more terrified of her than the fall.

"Yeah, well, whoever Daphne is, she's never gonna get her hands on you. You tried to kill my father and I'm gonna personally make sure you pay."

"She'll get to me," the judge cried out. "Daphne and her machete will get all of you."

"Don't be a fool," I said, extending my hand over the side of the railing. "Grab ahold of my hand and I'll pull you back up."

Just then the judge's foot slipped on the wet balcony, causing him to slide further down the railing. He has now supporting himself with his upper body alone, gripping tightly for dear life.

"I…I can't hold on," he cried out.

I leaned over the railing as far as I could, grabbing Judge Snodgrass by the forearms, and pulling with every ounce of strength I could. My back and shoulder muscles burning from the strain as I struggled to pull him onto the balcony.

The judge regained his footing, letting go of my right arm, before stabilizing himself on the railing.

"One more pull and you'll be over," I said.

"I told you, I'm not going to jail," he said, producing a blade and plunging it into my shoulder.

I reared back in pain, unable to keep hold of the judge and even though I tried to reach for him again, he was already plummeting toward the pavement below.

Trouble

"ATTENDANCE IS MANDATORY," Taxi said, after informing us we had been invited to the annual Marine Ball happening in four days.

I wasn't a dress kinda gal, ergo, I didn't own one, let alone a ball gown, and I had no interest or intention of complying with this bullshit edict. I raised my hand. "Tax—"

"Mandatory," he growled, and leaned in from his place at the head of the conference table. "Black tie."

He stood. "*Mandatory.*"

Stalking out of the room, he pulled the door closed with a TWAP behind him and I dropped my head to the table. "No," I whined to the floor. "No, no, no, no."

"Jette and Trouble," Dr. Fenton called out as the rest of my team let out varied versions of 'fuck.'

"Just kill me," I said, again to the floor.

"It's not all bad," Jette countered. "Any excuse to buy a new dress…"

"Ladies."

I raised my head and scowled at Dr. Fenton. "I'm no lady."

Dr. Fenton grinned. "Come on, you two. You're with me."

"Where are we going?" Jette asked.

"Shopping," Dr. Fenton replied.

"Nope," I snapped, with an emphasis on the 'P.' "I'm not going."

"Mandatory," Dr. Fenton parroted, her face hiding the smile her eyes couldn't.

"Why?" I cried. "It's not like I have anyone to impress."

"It's not about that," Dr. Fenton said.

"Then why can't I just go in my kutte?"

Jette gave me a look of horror and I rolled my eyes.

"Come on," Dr. Fenton repeated. "We've got the whole afternoon to find you a dress, shoes, and accoutrement."

"I don't have the money for a dress, shoes, and whatever that word means," I pointed out.

"Good thing you're not paying," she retorted.

"What? No." I waved my hand. "I'm nobody's charity case."

"Stephanie Palmer, you get your booty in my car, pronto, or I'm gonna sic Boots on you," Dr. Fenton warned and Jette burst out laughing.

"Shut it, Jette."

She just laughed harder. "Come on, girl*friend*, let's go spend all of Taxi's money."

I let out a hiss and pushed away from the table, following the women to my doom.

* * *

The night of the ball arrived, and I was a puddle of goo. But not the good kind that derives from being happy and in love. No, I was the Ghostbusters slime kind.

The dress I chose… no, that's not entirely true. Jette and Dr. Fenton forced me into this contraption, so this was on them. The dress *they* chose was a deep cherry red, fitted around the hips and legs, then flaring at the bottom. They called it a mermaid style. I called it fucking impossible to walk in. At least the top was criss-crossed and sleeveless so I could raise my arms in case I had to punch someone.

Jette had curled and swept my short hair back, ala Demi at the 1992 Oscars, and practically tied me to a chair in order to do my makeup, complete with red lipstick. At least she'd managed to hide my black eye.

I didn't look like myself and felt like a moron.

The worst part came when I had to put these strappy fucking heels on my feet. I had drawn a line in the sand when I almost fell walking across my room and shoved them back in the box. They didn't know it because my dress went to the floor, but I'd opted for a pair of Chucks instead.

I couldn't get away with not carrying a purse, however. I didn't have pockets to throw my cell phone and ID in, so I stuffed everything in a silver, sparkly clutch that matched the heels I'd discarded, then walked out of my dorm room to meet the car.

Jette was waiting for me out front and she grinned as

I tugged on my leather jacket and walked into the frigid air. "You just made it."

I wrinkled my nose. "Sorry. I had to make a quick adjustment."

We climbed into the car… well, I flopped in it as gracefully as I could, then the driver guided us to the venue a little over two miles away.

It was a particularly cold November, so I hoped I could leave my jacket on all night. My hopes would be dashed, however, when we walked into the room and my leather was virtually ripped from my body… by Jette.

"Hey, now," I snapped.

"Nice try."

"I'm cold."

"Then put some bandaids on your nipples and pretend you're in Fiji," she ordered, handing my jacket to some kid in a uniform.

I dropped my head and groaned. My nipples were set to high beam and I crossed my arms to hide them.

"You'll warm up," Jette assured me.

"I thought the whole point of these chicken cutlet, stick on titty hoisters was that they took care of this," I hissed.

"They would if we'd bought the right size," Jette hissed back. "You hide your jugs better than me." I scowled at her, but she just grinned. "Come on. Open bar means you won't care about your ta-tas for long."

She breezed away from me because she could. She wore a gorgeous, flower-child inspired sleeveless dress with a flowing skirt that faded from the deep blue on top into varying shades of blues as it went down.

I, on the other hand, had to waddle as gracefully as I could and keep up. Thank god I'd changed my shoes.

"Holy fuckballs," Tackle breathed out and I glared

up at him.

"Shut up," I snapped.

He pressed his lips into a thin line and grinned.

"Jesus," Boots hissed when he turned around. "You're a fuckin' babe."

"I swear to god, if one more comment is made, I will beat the shit out of all of you," I warned.

"Even me?"

My team parted and Doozer was suddenly in front of me. He wore a black tux, complete with deep red pocket hanky, and his kutte was nowhere to be seen.

He did, however, have on his boots, but they appeared to have been cleaned up for the occasion.

"What are you doing here?" I squeaked, and he closed the distance between us.

"You look beautiful," he rasped, cupping my face, and kissing me gently.

I felt a sting in the back of my nose and blinked back tears. "So do you."

He grinned. "You're the only person on earth who could get me out of my kutte."

"Apparently," I mused. "How…? Why…?"

"Taxi informed me about the ball, and the doc called to see if I had any ideas on what I'd like you to wear."

"Wait, what?" I gripped his tuxedo jacket. "You knew about the shopping torture?"

"He paid for it," Jette piped in, and Doozer frowned.

"That was supposed to be confidential."

"Oh, whoops. Sorry," she said, not looking at all sorry.

"You paid for this getup?" I accused.

"Baby, there was no way in hell I was lettin' another man pay for my woman's dress. So I told the doc I'd like to see you in red, and she did not disappoint. You are fuckin' stunning."

"You came all the way here just to see me in a red dress?"

"Yes and no." He chuckled. "We'll talk about that later."

"Can we talk about it now…. back at the dorms?"

"No way in hell," he said.

I wrinkled my nose. "You can't possibly be comfortable in that monkey suit," I said, sliding my hands up his chest.

"Ooh, careful of my right shoulder," Doozer said, wincing.

"What's the matter? What happened?"

"I'm okay, but I was sort of…well…stabbed."

"Stabbed? Like with a knife?"

"A letter opener," he replied. "Made of solid fourteen-carat gold."

"What? Who stabbed you with a gold letter opener?"

"Judge Snodgrass. Apparently, it was as a birthday gift from his secretary."

"Who's Judge Snodgrass?"

"Baby, so much has happened since we last spoke, I barely know where to begin, and I promise I will fill you in on every detail but tonight is about you."

"Are you sure you're okay?"

"I have the prettiest girl in the world on my arm, I'm gonna put aside my discomfort and show you off. Besides, we have all the time in the world to get caught up."

"How long are you here?" I asked.

"Forever."

I snorted. "Oh, okay."

"I am."

I frowned. "What do you mean?"

"We're transferring to the Savannah chapter."

"What do you mean, we?" I demanded.

"You need to be close to the team, I need to be close to you, so Minus and Taxi made a deal and compromised with Savannah. We are both patching over… together. That is, if that's what you want."

I could no longer hold back the tears. "Are you serious?"

"Yeah, honey. Are you okay with that?"

"Hell, yes, I'm okay with that." I gripped the lapels of his jacket again. "We really get to be together?"

"We really get to be together," he confirmed, and leaned down to kiss me again. "Now, you ready to dance with me, slow like?"

"I'm so, so ready to dance with you, slow like."

He grinned, wrapping an arm around me, and guiding me onto the dance floor.

As I slipped my hand into his, he held me close and we rocked together as couples waltzed around us. Neither Doozer nor I knew how to dance, so we just let our love for each other dictate our rhythm.

I couldn't believe how incredibly blessed I'd been with this epic love, but I knew in my bones I would never take it for granted.

Trouble

One year later…

I WALKED INTO the Burning Saints Sanctuary on the outskirts of Savannah and headed straight for the kitchen. I had a six-pack of beer and it needed to be chilled before the family night tonight.

"Hey, Trouble," Ronnie said as she walked into the room just as I slid the beer into the fridge.

Ronnie was Zaius's old lady. Zaius had been the Savannah chapter president for almost as long as Cutter, god rest his soul, had been president out in Portland. Now that Minus had taken over Portland, it was an adjustment transitioning from the new class of biker back to old school. At least, I was used to Cowboy, but Doozer had a bigger culture shock than I did.

Well… sort of.

There had apparently been a bit of a hard sell situation when it came to me being part of the Savannah chapter. Zaius was old-school and women in MCs wasn't something he thought was a good idea. But both Minus and Zaius wanted Doozer in Savannah and Doozer was very clear we were a package deal, so Zaius had relented.

It took me a few weeks not to feel like I was only there because my man was the valuable commodity and that was mostly due to Ronnie. That's not to say Doozer didn't try to put my mind at ease, but he was a phenomenal artist when it came to custom bike builds and the Saints were having a hard time keeping up with the demand. A mechanic, no matter how good, was somewhat a dime a dozen, but I had something none of them had.

A vagina.

And a way of speaking to my fellow sisterhood that was not mansplaining, so it actually didn't take long to show the other bikers that I was needed.

I had originally planned to just sit back and do my thing quietly under the radar, but Ronnie had suggested a different way, and that way was to shove my femininity in their faces, while showing them my mechanical prowess. It had worked, and the brothers had come around a little faster than I expected.

And although I couldn't prove it, I think Ronnie had also worked behind the scenes to make the transition easier for Zaius, which in turn trickled down to the men.

I could not, however, get out of wearing the bracelet

all the old ladies wore. It had a panic button with built-in tracking device. Should anything happen to one of us, our men would be able to find us immediately. I had no idea how Taxi would feel about this piece of tech strapped to me at all times, but I figured what he didn't know wouldn't kill him.

Since Doozer was all about equal rights, he wore one as well, although, he didn't mention it to the men. His looked quite a bit different than mine, so no one had questioned him about it, and we kept it between us.

"Hi, Ronnie," I said, hugging her. "How are you?"

"If I was better, it'd be illegal."

"Love it." I grinned. "Have you seen Doozer?"

"He's in the meeting room."

I nodded and headed that way.

I'd been at the dreaded gynecologist all morning getting my annual, so I'd planned on meeting Doozer here instead of our new home. He'd picked up the keys this morning and I couldn't wait to move in.

After all the drama with Judge Snodgrass, Doozer was looking forward to making a fresh start far away from Portland. The relationship between Doozer and his father had grown into something quite unexpected in the wake of the attempt on his life. He and Doozer spoke every week on the phone and Doozer was even helping him plan his cross-country RV trip.

In the months after Judge Snodgrass' death, a pile of dirty laundry surfaced regarding his dealings with the criminal underworld. Falling to his death was likely the easy road considering the list of criminal charges he would have faced. With Snodgrass gone, the Beast's plan was dead in the water, but they'd be back, and we'd be ready.

It had taken us a month to find what I hoped would be our forever home. Three bedrooms, two bathrooms, giant great room and kitchen on two acres with a shop. All this space meant we had room to grow and I couldn't wait to have little Mancini babies running around.

The door was open, so I knocked on the wood as I walked inside, and all chatter stopped. Doozer sat on the edge of the table, head bowed over his phone as Squirrel and Taz oohed and ahhed over whatever he was showing them.

"Hi," I said, and Doozer grinned, sliding his phone in his pocket.

"Hey. Perfect timing."

"Oh, yeah?" I asked, as he closed the distance between us and leaned down for a kiss.

Squirrel and Taz gave me chin lifts as they scurried out of the room. Squirrel was at an equal level to me and Doozer, but Taz was our sergeant, so he was a little more standoffish.

"Something I said?" I retorted.

Doozer chuckled. "I've got a surprise for you. You up to following, or do you want to ride bitch?"

"Oh, I'm always up to being your bitch," I sassed. "But it depends on where we're going."

"Home."

"Yes," I hissed. "I'll follow."

"Great. Let's go."

I clapped my hands and followed him out to our bikes. We drove the short ten minutes to our new home, and it was even prettier than it had been a week ago. I was so excited, I felt my heart race as we parked in front and set our helmets on the seats.

Doozer held his hand out to me and I jogged to catch up to him and link my fingers with his. He held the house keys up and jangled them before unlocking the door, then lifting me in his arms. "I love you, Stephanie

Palmer."

"I love you too, Marco Mancini."

He grinned and kissed me as he carried me over the threshold and set me on my feet. I glanced around the room, my eyes coming to rest on a giant fish tank in the corner of what would be our dining room.

"What the…?" I breathed out and stalked over to it. "These are discus."

"They are," Doozer confirmed.

"Where did you find them?" I leaned down so I could watch the cutest pair of fish dance through the water.

"Cowboy helped me get them here. They're from Dr. Sniffy."

"Wait, what?"

"They're Bonnie and Clyde's fry."

"Oh my god, seriously?" I squeaked, my eyes flooding with tears.

"Seriously," he confirmed, wrapping his arms around me. "I have tentatively called them Sam and Molly, but we can change the nam—"

"Don't you dare," I said, bursting into a full-blown sobbing fest at the mention of my favorite movie characters. Particularly since Patrick Swayze was no longer on the earth, so in some ways, true life was imitating art which made things so much more bittersweet.

Doozer chuckled gently as he pulled me tighter against him. "So if I told you I may want to take up pottery, would you be up to that?"

"Stop it," I blubbered out. "You had me at 'fry.' I can't believe you remembered the correct term for baby fish."

"I remember everything when it comes to you."

I nodded. "Yeah, I'm figuring that out."

He kissed me again, then dropped his forehead to

mine. “You are so fuckin’ amazing, baby.”

“Back atya.”

“Thank you for Sam and Molly.” I turned back toward the fish tank, leaning down to get a closer look.

“You’re welcome.”

I faced him again, my eyes seeing nothing until I looked down to find him on one knee, holding up a diamond solitaire ring.

“Shut up!” I squeaked, slapping my hands over my face. “Get up.”

“Will you marry me?”

I slapped his arm. “No, get up.”

“No, you won’t marry me?” he challenged.

“Yes, I’ll marry you, but only if you get up off your knees.”

He slid the ring on my finger and finally stood, wrapping his arms around me. “You’re so lucky you said yes.”

I laughed. “Well, we’ve already signed our lives away with this house, so we’re already forever entwined. Probably a good idea to make it official.”

“I love being forever entwined with you, baby.”

“Me too,” I said, kissing him again.

The doorbell pealed and I pulled away from Doozer with a frown. “Who the hell is that?”

He grimaced. “The movers.”

“Movers? What movers?” I demanded. “We don’t have anything to move.”

“Ronnie and Jules did a little shopping.”

Jules was Wingman’s wife, and she was a ballbuster in the best of ways. Wingman was our very gruff, very scary enforcer with a heart of gold. Only, he didn’t show that heart to most people.

“No,” I breathed out.

“Yes,” he countered, releasing me, and heading for

the door.

He pulled it open and Ronnie and Jules strolled in, followed by bikers carrying boxes and furniture.

"Glad you've got your clothes on," Ronnie said, hugging Doozer, then me.

"Five more minutes…" I retorted, and she laughed.

"The club has bought you your bedroom set," she said. "We know you've got nothing just yet, but you have to have a place to sleep and after much arm twisting, Doozer gave us the link to the set you've been eyeing."

"But that was almost ten-grand," I whispered.

"We know," she whispered back.

"Oh my god, Ronnie. Thank you."

"You're welcome." She grinned, holding up a six-pack of beer. "Now show me to the fridge and let these boys work."

I blushed and led her and Jules into the kitchen.

"I don't have dishes," I admitted. "But how about I order pizza?"

"That sounds great," Jules said.

As the men hauled all of the heavy boxes and parts up to our bedroom, I sat with Jules and Ronnie in the kitchen and drank beer while we waited for the pizza.

Before our food arrived, however, several of the other club women arrived carrying bags of groceries and cheap dishes to 'tide us over' until we could buy what we wanted.

Before the night was over, I'd had to excuse myself at least sixty-two times to wipe away tears I'd been trying to hide most of the evening.

I couldn't believe how incredibly welcome and loved I felt, and I couldn't wait to spend the rest of my life with Doozer and our new family.

By the time everyone filed out of our house, however, I was horny as hell and needed to christen the bed.

"Meet me upstairs?" I said in my best come hither voice.

Doozer met my eyes with a grin almost wider than his face. "Yes, ma'am."

While he locked up the house, I rushed upstairs, grabbing my overnight bag I would not let anyone else touch, dropping it on the bed. I pulled out the nipple clamps I'd stowed in there holding them up just as Doozer walked into the room. I'd bought these particular toys myself and it had shocked the hell out of both of us when I discovered I like them so much. So much in fact, I was contemplating actually piercing my nipples. I hadn't quite gotten up the nerve to do that yet, but it was still in the maybe pile.

"Oh, ho, you want to play," he deduced.

"Hell, yes, I want to play."

We rushed to divest ourselves of our clothing, then I pushed Doozer onto the bed, straddling him with a grin. He was rock hard as I wrapped my hand around his dick and guided it inside of me. I lowered myself, then braced my hands on his chest as I lifted my hips, then slid down again.

"You gonna go that slow all night?" he teased.

"I'm priming the pump."

"How about you let me take over and fuck you until you can't walk."

"If you want me to shut my mouth, I'd suggest you grab the clamps and fuck me from behind."

He tweaked my nipple with a grin. "Yes, ma'am."

Sliding gently out of me, he retrieved the nipple clamps off the nightstand while I positioned myself on all-fours.

He reached under my body to clamp me, then slapped my pussy. "Spread wider, Trouble."

I spread wider and his fingers dipped inside of me

before slapping my pussy again. I whimpered as I felt the flood, loving what he could do to my body.

He slid two fingers inside of me again, before replacing them with his dick, then one of his fingers pressed against my tight hole.

"Oh, god, yes," I hissed, and he pressed it into me.

I almost came right then and there, but he started to move, his finger matching the rhythm of his hips as he fucked me.

"Doozer," I whimpered as my body thrummed with need.

"Don't come."

"I… oh, god," I whispered.

He removed the finger from my ass and gripped my hips, slamming harder and harder until I could no longer hold myself together, screaming his name as an orgasm washed over me, and I collapsed on the bed.

He thrust twice more and then I felt his dick pulse as he rolled us to our sides in a spoon fashion, tugging the clamps from my nipples.

I reached back and grabbed his thigh as I worked hard to catch my breath. "I'm gonna need you to buy lube."

He let out a quiet hiss. "Come again?"

I chuckled. "Yes, I plan to. Often. Especially if you buy lube and we try that again with your dick instead of your finger."

"Jesus fucking Christ are you serious?"

"Hell, yes," I breathed out.

"Okay, baby, I'll buy the lube."

I laughed. "Of course, you will."

"I need to buy you a house more often."

I grinned as I worked to catch my breath. "It was the fish, honey, not the house."

"Well, then I'll buy you more fuckin' fish."

I rolled onto him, kissing his neck just over his spiderweb tattoo. "I love you."

"Love you too, baby."

"Up for another go?"

He laughed. "Fuck, yeah, I'm up for another go. *If* you ride me."

I grinned, sitting up and straddling him. We made love for another hour before falling into oblivion wrapped up in each other.

I had found my forever and I was never going to let him go.

FISHBOWL COCKTAIL

Coconut Rum
Vodka
Sweet and Sour Mix
Blue Curaçao
Peach Schnapps
Pineapple Juice
Sprite
Swedish Fish
Ice
Maraschino Cherry
Pineapple Wedge
Nerds

1. Fill a cocktail shaker about half full of ice.
2. Add the rum, vodka, sour mix, pineapple juice, curaçao, and schnapps to the shaker and shake
3. Add Nerds to the bottom of two individual bowls, then add ice and Swedish (arrange them so the ice holds the fish against the bowl for presentation
4. Strain the contents of the cocktail shaker evenly into the bowls.
5. Top with club soda and garnish with fruit.

USA Today Bestselling Author Jack Davenport is a true romantic at heart, but he has a rebel's soul. His writing is passionate, energetic, and often fueled by his true life, fiery romance with author wife, Piper Davenport.

Twenty-five years as a professional musician lends a unique perspective into the world of rock stars, while his outlaw upbringing gives an authenticity to his MC series.

Like Jack's FB page and get to know him!
(www.facebook.com/jackdavenportauthor)

Made in the USA
Columbia, SC
25 February 2023

12955736R00126